The Eagle
&
the Monk

Seven Principles of
Successful Change

THE EAGLE
&
THE MONK

Seven Principles of
Successful Change

William A. Jenkins
Richard W. Oliver

G&B
GATES & BRIDGES
A Division of United Publishers Group

Gates & Bridges
A Division of United Publishers Group Inc.
50 Washington Street
Norwalk, CT 06854

Library of Congress Cataloging-in-Publication Data

Jenkins, William A.
    The eagle and the monk   : seven principles of successful
change / William A. Jenkins, Richard W. Oliver.
        p.   cm.
    ISBN 0-8038-9405-8
    1. Organizational change — Fiction. I. Oliver, Richard W.,
    1946– . II. Title.
    PS3560.E5144E24 1998
    913'.54 — DC21   97-26871
                                                                    CIP

Printed in the United States of America.

10 9 8 7 6 5 4 3 2 1

Contents

Acknowledgments

We are convinced that the eagle and the monk could not have handled the change in their lives without the feedback from the many companies, family, friends, and colleagues who encouraged them to the conclusion of their plight. Therefore, we would like to thank those who supported us with their comments as we created *The Eagle & the Monk*: Nelson Andrews, Jeff Benson, Russell W. Brothers III, Gerry Butters, Peter Coholan, Nancy Cox, Carter Crenshaw, Donna Culver, Peter Dawkins, Terry Deal, Townes Duncan, Colin Eller, Kathy Eller, Cherrill Farnsworth, Steve Fuchs, Rick Gibson, Phyliss Gobbell, Jon Gullette, Ed Gurowitz, Rich Heckman, Eko and Toshinari Ishii, Donna C. Kane, Fletcher Lance, Bob Lane, Michael Lewis, Clifford W. Licko, Howard Lipman, Lee Ann Mann, Rich McDaniel, Ben McSwiney, Gerry Moersdorf, Jr., Ann Neely, Qinglin (Austin) Na, Carrie Oliver, Dave Putnam, Bob Reid, Courtney Reynolds, Tim Richardson, Christi Royer, Carole Runyeon, Roger Saunders, M. D. Seo, Ellie Shick, Larry Shoaf, Jim Smith, Kim Spelden, Fred Talbott, Tamiyo and Gordon Togasski, Cal Turner, Bill Tym, and those who we may have inadvertently left out. We are most appreciative of your efforts.

We would especially like to acknowledge *The Eagle & the Monk* "team" for their continuous hard work: Craig Andrews, Kim Brothers, Ruth Ann Brown, Rita Carswell, Jimmy D'Andrea, Jill Gabbe, Paige Henke, Mary Ann Jenkins, Danielle Mezera, Elmear K. O'Connell, Susan Oliver, Sarah Randel, Jamie Reeves, Jeannie Rice, and Mike Schoenfeld. Thank you! Your creativity, encouragement, endless energy, and special gifts brought real meaning to one of our principles—team synergy.

Of course without our agent, Peter Miller, and his right-hand man, Yuri Skujins, there would be no need for these acknowledgments. Thank you for believing in *The Eagle & the Monk* and for selecting Henno Lohmeyer, our publisher. Thank you, Henno, for presenting *The Eagle & the Monk* in the beautiful format it deserves and thanks to your staff for bringing *The Eagle & the Monk* to this point.

And finally, our readers. Thank you for reading *The Eagle & the Monk*. We hope you feel the passion that we felt and still feel. Our goal was to have something you could finish in approximately two hours. Further, we endeavored to create something useful for anyone undergoing change, not just business professionals. It is our hope that you will make the inevitable and continual process of change in your life successful, using the Seven Principles as a guide. Happy reading and we hope all the changes you make are successful.

September 1997
William A. Jenkins
Richard W. Oliver

Introduction

This book is about change, the fundamental, unalterable force of our times. More importantly, it is about how we as individuals and organizations deal with change.

With nearly sixty years of experience between us as leaders in large successful organizations, and as students of leadership, change, and strategic management, we have concluded that change, or more precisely the "management" of change, is today the common denominator of concern for virtually every individual and organization. Our work with and for many individuals and organizations has reinforced our strong belief that it is the approach to managing change, not change itself, that makes the critical difference between success and failure.

As we began our research on change, we recognized that there was much more to change than we could ever know, even with a lifetime of study. While there is much we still seek to know about, of one thing we are sure: Change is inevitable. Whether in small insignificant ways, or dramatic, life-altering ways, change is, today, affecting every aspect of life.

Change knows no boundaries, and it respects no traditions. Change can happen instantaneously and by force, or it can happen slowly, almost imperceptibly, over a long period of time. It has no schedule to follow.

Change fears nothing, yet it is feared. Many times, change can be painful. If given a choice, most of us choose the familiar over the unknown that change so often brings with it. Change can bring bad fortune, but it can, just as often, improve our institutions, organizations, relationships, and our personal well-being.

Why do we, as individuals and collectively as organizations, fear change so much? Why does the very mention of the word "change" so often create such high levels of anxiety? In the organizations with which we deal, and the people who populate them, we have found two overarching qualities that, when present, accelerate the successful adaptation to change and, when absent, often create paralyzing fear and slow, painful periods of adjustment. In thoughtful, careful analysis of successful individual and organizational change, these two qualities ultimately surface as the defining difference.

The first quality is the acknowledgment of worth—of self and of others. Far too frequently, we have seen that worth, in individual and organizational terms, take on a material or financial dimension that denigrates the inherent value of the individual. Organizations dealing most successfully with change are those that have been able to preserve and enshrine the role of the individual through acknowledgment of worth.

We have also come to understand, however, that no one in today's environment can succeed alone, that success presupposes critical interdependencies. It is in the quality, the very fabric of any relationship . . . in teams at work, in small groups at church, in marriage, or between large companies or countries . . . that change tests us most. For relationships to withstand the assault of change, we must have trust.

In our study of change and its successful management, we have discovered that the acknowledgment of worth is the fundamental precondition to the development of trust and that trust is the foundation of any successful adaptation to change.

In the story that follows, we will discuss these themes more fully and demonstrate how the seven principles of successful change can be put to use by individuals and organizations to build a climate of trust based on the acknowledgment of worth.

SEVEN PRINCIPLES OF
SUCCESSFUL CHANGE

1. *Accept your worth, acknowledge others' worth.* Every person has worth, including you. Accept your worth and acknowledge the worth of others around you. Accepting and acknowledging worth provides the foundation of successful change.

2. *Generate trust.* When there is trust between two or more people, change is more readily accepted. Being trusted and trusting others allows you and others to be positive, productive individuals. Trust is a centerpiece of successful change.

3. *Learn by empathy.* Those who continuously learn about themselves, others, work, and life have a greater capacity for change. By observing others, broadening interests, and understanding different perspectives, you can gain an instinctive understanding about change. Connect to change by daily learning.

4. *Embrace change.* Change is inevitable and appears to be increasing at exponential rates. You can either resist change or accept it. Since your life is simply a series of changes, yield to change.

5. *Unleash the synergy.* Team synergy is the result of two or more people valuing and trusting each other. When two or more people produce ideas, they ultimately make improvements that are significantly greater than would have been possible separately.

6. *Discover champions, depend on masters, find a sage.* Effective change will be steered by more than a leader. The environment of change will eliminate autocratic supervision. Instead, it will seek champions, masters, and sages to foster change.

7. *Liberate decision-making.* Change resulting from one person's decisions rarely works. Share decision-making with those around you—empower them. Ownership in decisions promotes change.

FINALLY, WHY A FABLE?

Our goal is to quickly and dramatically communicate our message about change with the sense of urgency. We feel that a fable best conveys the excitement we feel about the seven principles and their power to help successfully manage change.

Fables, parables, and the like have been used since the beginning of time to communicate ideas in a powerful and compelling way. It is our hope that this fable will contribute to a greater understanding of the unrelenting changes we believe will be a permanent part of the future.

And so, we begin our story of the eagle and the monk . . .

1. The Monk

Gentle tears rolled down her once-smooth face as Shizuka Kiyoki fastened the ceremonial obi around her funeral kimono. Married some forty years to Akira, she rose early this day to send him on his final journey to the hereafter.

A quiet man, respectful of tradition, he was honored by his fellow workers and his many friends. As well he should be, she thought. He was dedicated to his work, those with whom he worked, and his company. He spent so much time with his work that he was almost married to it rather than me.

But that is the Japanese way, and I will not complain, Shizuka thought. No one would listen to me if I did, and I would only diminish his memory.

"He was a man of his times and of his culture; he did what he had to do, and I will honor that," she spoke aloud, although there was no one near to hear the words.

Despite Akira's lifelong dedication to his work, she, and she alone, knew that he would rather have given his life to the quiet contemplation of a monk—to think deeply on the Japanese tradition and to reflect on history, as well as to live it. And live it he did, she thought.

Akira had been a direct participant in much of twentieth-century Japanese history. His mother, although Japanese, was born and raised in China, and her family had been part of the early Japanese settlements in Manchuria.

His father, a young Japanese businessman, had met his mother while stationed in China in his first overseas assignment. They married and returned to Japan just months before Akira (meaning enlightened one) was born. His younger brother, Shinji, was the second to join the young Kiyoki family, two years after his father returned from the first great war.

As a young man, Akira loved history and art—especially the history and art of ancient Japan. His tutor was his mother, Moma-san, who was discovering much of her heritage for the first time herself. She had never been in her native country until her marriage, and she took young Akira to most of the thousand shrines and temples of Kyoto. Kyoto was, until modern times, the political capital of Japan. It was now the center of Japan's cultural heritage.

Their most frequent visits were to Nijojo Castle (the Kyoto home of the Tokugawa shogun who united Japan after many years of internal conflict). They visited so often, in fact, that Akira envisioned for himself a life of protecting Japanese traditions as the official keeper of some important icon that symbolized his country's strength and heritage.

As a child, he and Shinji spent countless hours with Moma-san. His father was a businessman employed by a major Japanese zaibatsu, a group of large interlocked firms. His father spent most of his waking hours with his business associates, working long hours during the day and then talking and drinking with customers till the late hours of the night. Such was the custom of the Japanese "salaryman."

In moments of tranquillity, his mother would teach Akira and his brother the sacred Chinese art form of calligraphy. Although he enjoyed sports as much as his younger brother, it was Akira who developed the deepest reverence for the kanji, or the Chinese character. Kanji is the most difficult, but most important, of the three alphabets used in written Japanese. Unlike his brother, he spent countless hours perfecting his brush stroke.

He became so proficient that many began to believe his hand had great promise. He was even able to sell much of his calligraphy at local fairs and celebrations. For Akira, it was the integration of all things Japanese, and he relished this skill.

An excellent scholar, Akira finished his rigorous Japanese high school work near the very top of his class and was accepted at Todai, the prestigious University of Tokyo, into its Japanese history program. He delayed his departure for the university for two years, as he was invited to study calligraphy with an aging monk and calligrapher who was to take one last student. Akira learned much from his *sensei*, and he was saddened by the relatively short time they had together. Nevertheless, he looked forward to the university.

However, the December before he was to leave for Tokyo, the military forces of Japan attacked Pearl Harbor. By March, in the final weeks before his departure for school, Akira decided that he must set aside personal goals to serve his country.

Shortly after beginning his military service, his superiors discovered that he spoke passable Chinese. So Akira was assigned to a communication section of an army combat unit heading for China.

Toward the end of the war, his unit took heavy casualties. Akira rose in the ranks by virtue of the sheer loss of his troop's numbers and because of his increasing knowledge of the communications gear that he used daily. He eventually became a low-ranking officer.

Despite almost daily damage to the communication equipment and a severe lack of new replacement parts,

Akira was able to keep his field commander in touch with the central command post.

Their unit spent the final exhausting months of the war in constant motion, evading the enemy in what most now knew was a losing, futile effort. However, Akira found that his newly discovered technical competency matched his growing fluency with the Chinese language.

Several days after the Japanese surrender, his unit, unaware of the peace, was still maneuvering about the Chinese countryside. A unit of Chinese Communist militia, led by Russian advisors, was in close pursuit. In a small pass in the mountains, most of his unit was destroyed in a surprise attack by the enemy.

Akira was hit by mortar fire and awoke many hours later amid a mass of groaning and writhing bodies on a train bound for a Chinese prisoner-of-war camp located near the Russian border.

His right hand, the hand that had spent so many hours in the reverent practice of calligraphy, was badly damaged and throbbing intensely. He knew he needed treatment, and soon, if he was ever to use it again.

But it was not to be. They traveled many days aboard the train without food or rest. Conditions in the camp were equally deplorable, and medical assistance was scarcer than solid food. After two years with no rice or meat, his body was as badly damaged as was his spirit. He worried more about his spirit, numbed by the endless boredom and isolation from his homeland, and the knowledge that his hand, although healed, would never again hold a brush.

One morning, which at first was like so many others, changed dramatically when a Chinese political official came to the camp. He was, apparently, of some stature. The prison guards, whose attention to detail had all but disappeared and whose dress had deteriorated and become slovenly, suddenly sprang to attention. After a brief ceremony of flag raising, the official addressed the captured Japanese soldiers with a long political speech, which Akira was forced to translate. He announced to the troops that, despite their crimes, they were free to go.

Their stunned disbelief turned to bewilderment when the official also informed the prisoners that the Chinese government would not provide transportation and that they would have to walk home.

In the two years of captivity, Akira had become an unofficial leader among the soldiers and was sought after for his wisdom and strength. Although more senior officers remained officially in command, when survival was at stake, the men always gravitated to Akira because of his mental toughness and knowledge of Chinese ways.

As they walked out of China and across the Korean peninsula to the port of Inchon where an American warship would take them home, many of Akira's comrades died and were buried where they fell. Akira was determined that he would get home after suffering so much. He was not yet ready to join his ancestors.

As they drew closer to Japan day by day, Akira felt a

gradual shift of leadership back to the more senior officers. The officers and the men were returning to their
old ways. The leadership that he had enjoyed in the
camp was disappearing as they neared their homeland.

Once aboard the American warship, the USS
Cherokee, Akira again assumed his place as a traditional
Japanese soldier, one of the many joining this ship from
various parts of Asia for the return home.

As he didn't speak their language, he had little con-
tact with the American sailors. Many of these sailors,
Akira found out from his comrades who spoke English,
had not been involved in the war. They had joined their
navy near the end of the war and had been stationed in
Japan only recently. On the deck of the great ship, he
stood at the rail and was watching Korea disappear in
the mist of the Yellow Sea when he became aware of a
presence beside him.

A young American sailor, not much younger than
himself, stood at his side smoking a cigarette. He turned
to Akira and studied him with a wry smile. After several
seconds of silence, he said something incomprehensible
to Akira and offered him a cigarette.

It was Akira's first cigarette in over two years. The
sailor spoke again, but Akira understood nothing. Lighting
the cigarette for him, the sailor tried once again to communicate with him, then, realizing the futility, laughed
a friendly laugh.

Despite his lack of understanding, Akira laughed too.
Then tears filled his eyes, tears of relief, of hope, of joy,

and tears of a brief friendship. Soon the Japanese soldiers were being called to eat, and he left the American alone at the rail, not seeing him again during the short voyage home.

During their brief encounter, Akira had tried to keep his badly mangled right hand hidden from the American, using his left hand to smoke. As he turned to leave, however, the American noticed the damage to Akira's right hand and tried to stop him. But Akira was quickly lost among the mass of men on deck.

Later, Akira described the markings of the American soldier's uniform to one of his English-speaking comrades and found that the American was a man of rank, a lieutenant, and highly regarded among the American sailors.

Arriving in Japan, Akira's thoughts now turned to his family. He had heard no news of his family since months before his capture, and he did not know if they had survived—or if they had survived, would they know he was coming home?

His fears were unfounded. When he reached Kyoto, he found his parents at the train station, alerted to his return by officials in Tokyo. At home, his father, too old to fight in this war, seemed broken in defeat and was still mourning for Akira's brother, Shinji, who had died at Corregidor. However, like most Japanese, his father silently, and without bitterness, accepted those who had conquered them and now occupied their country.

Akira rested for several months after his return, while

his body regained its strength, and the lingering images of war and thoughts of survival turned to those of the future.

Despite the urging of his mother, Akira chose not to go to the university. He was not sure his family could afford it; furthermore, he thought he had seen too much of life firsthand to lock himself away in contemplation of the past.

Instead, he joined a company located just outside Kyoto, manufacturing the heavy machinery so necessary for the reconstruction of postwar Japan. It had been in business before the war, but during the war the factory had been converted to the production of military equipment.

They were, with the help of the American military, building a new factory. The original factory had escaped major structural damage during the air raids, because the Americans did not bomb Kyoto. However, the plant had been ravished near the end of the war, first by desperate soldiers looking for war materiel, and then by equally desperate civilians who tore away at its wooden structure seeking firewood.

Although it was the Japanese custom to work in one place for one's entire life, Akira thought he might stay a year or two at this work until he could earn enough yen to travel and see the world. However, he was soon an integral member of the work team that became an important part of his life.

He was unable to do much physical work due to his

damaged right hand, so he was assigned initially to the design group rebuilding the factory. Despite an eventual move to the manufacturing team, he retained a lifelong interest in plant design and construction. As so many of the company's former employees never returned from the war, Akira quickly rose in seniority to be a manufacturing team leader. The technical and leadership skills he had learned in the army now served him well. Eventually, he was earning enough to marry Shizuka, in a marriage arranged by his father.

Akira and Shizuka grew to love each other very much. Soon there were children, and Akira took on the role of father, as well as husband, to complement his growing responsibilities at work. He was determined to spend more time with his children than his father had spent with him. Each year, however, the company did better and better, and eventually their products were of such quality and value that they were sold, not just in Japan, but around the world. The company was very successful, and with that success, Akira found himself spending most of his waking hours at the plant.

At some point, Akira realized that he had more than enough money to travel the world, but by then, family and work responsibilities overshadowed any travel considerations. Alas, his dream to see the world never materialized.

✻   ✻   ✻

He made a good life for us, Shizuka thought, as she made final preparations before her children would take her to the temple for Akira's funeral. He worked hard, particularly in those early years when Japan lacked so much. He struggled and learned the ways of the West, with their modern technologies and ways of doing business. She recalled in her mind the year he swelled with pride as his company won the Deming Award, the most coveted business award in Japan. In fact, she thought, as she smiled to herself, he was more proud of that award than the fact that he had become an important contributor to the design of many of the new areas of the plant.

Akira became a vocal champion of the highly skilled Japanese worker, both in the plant and to any that would listen outside it. During the infrequent periods of unrest between the workers and management, he became the center of conciliation and compromise.

Returning home late each night from the plant, he spent the remainder of most evenings helping his son and daughter with their school work. Although not required to do so, he worked most Saturdays. Sundays, however, were reserved for visiting the temples and shrines of Kyoto, exposing his family to the rich traditions of Japan as his mother had done for him.

Late in the evening, his family asleep, Akira would study the history and traditions of his people, and with his left hand, practice the calligraphy that he would allow no one, even Shizuka, to see. At first he tried to use his right hand, but he eventually gave up as it would not hold the brush correctly, even when the brush was strapped in place. He felt his left-handed efforts were inferior to his prewar calligraphy, but it refreshed his

soul and focused his mind as he practiced the more difficult strokes.

Following his retirement from the company at age
sixty, he happily spent the next twenty-one years as a
groundskeeper in a Shinto shrine near his home.

"My husband, I know nothing of the hereafter,"
Shizuka spoke aloud and in her most reverent voice,
"but I hope you find time there to be that which you
always wished to be."

It was steel cold later that day as Shizuka slowly
climbed the long stairs of the Buddhist temple, one of
the oldest in Kyoto. Carrying the calligraphy scrolls
that had remained hidden from her until his death,
Shizuka smiled bravely to herself as she recalled her
husband's oft repeated reflection on what it meant to
be Japanese:

"We're a strange people, we Japanese.
When it comes to either religion or business, we
    borrow the best from others and make it our own.
We're born Shinto, our native religion.
We marry Christian, a tradition borrowed from the
    West.
Then, we die Buddhist, something we learned from
    the Chinese.
And in business, we're pragmatists, too.
We take the best from anywhere and make it part of
    our Japanese way.
It's our strength as a people, the secret of our
    success. It is our special history."

On this day, a day when Akira would join his revered ancestors, Shizuka wondered if her husband of so many years would still feel the same about the future of the Japanese people.

Just as she neared the end of her climb, she looked up to see a magnificent bird. It was dark brown in color, almost black, and many times larger than any bird she had ever seen before. The bird seemed to eye her closely as it circled the temple, completely blocking her from the sun.

The giant bird hesitated just briefly, then flew swiftly in the direction of the sea, leaving only the sight of its white-tipped feathers in view.

*   *   *

As consciousness slowly formed in the void behind his eyes, his first thoughts were of the hard, flat surface on which he lay. As more coherence began to fill the emptiness that seemed to engulf him, his first rational thought was that he was cold, very cold, and quite possibly naked. . . .

He lay still for what felt like a century, trying to make some sense of where he was—and of things long past. But now he was alert, completely awake, and acutely aware of his surroundings.

Through the cobwebs of his thoughts, he began to remember a little of his former life but not of how he came to be here.

Later he would contemplate how he got to this barren place. Right now he wanted to get up from the cold, gray rock that was his bed and find something to clothe and warm his shivering body.

He didn't have to look far, because as he rose, he found a neatly folded stack of coarse, dark cloth at his feet. Picking it up, he realized that it was the simple garb of a monk—plain, functional, and with a cord belt.

Quickly he pulled it over his head, and despite its coarseness, he sensed that it was made especially for him. It felt wonderfully warm and precisely tailored to fit his body. He deftly slipped his feet into the leather sandals cradled under the robe, and found to his surprise that even they seemed to be shaped to the contours of his feet. Despite their simple design and sparse leather, the sandals warmed him completely.

In the demanding time of his "other life," he had often daydreamed of being a monk. Now he wondered if the clothes he wore made him so.

In these clothes I will live the life of a monk, he thought, even though I will miss my work and the simple pleasures of family life. As much as his family, he would miss his work and the meaning it gave his life.

Perhaps I have no choice but to be a monk, he reflected, as I do not know this place nor the circumstances of my coming here.

He felt a gentle, warm breeze caress his face, but for some mystical reason, he knew the wind bore him no good. It was a wind of warning, and he knew that one day soon he would need to confront it. Despite the warmth of his garments, his body shuddered as if in forewarning.

"How I deal with this wind will also wait for later contemplation," he said aloud. "First, I must determine where I am, and if possible, if there is any way home from this barren place."

He struggled up the rock behind him as it seemed to lead to higher ground. As he had so often told his group, in a life that now seemed remote and long ago, "Always seek the high ground to gain perspective on your situation. Although the present is important, only a long-term vision will guide you safely into the future."

Atop the rock, he could see for miles in every direction. He was on an island, an island of rocks—cold, shiny and gray, much like the one upon which he now stood. The island was surrounded by blue-green water that looked both inviting and treacherous. He knew immediately that there was nowhere to go. "This old body can still swim many miles," he said aloud, "but in which direction and to what place?"

Finally, he concluded: There is no means of escape. There is nothing.

His thoughts jumped rapidly back and forth, from the forbiddance of his surroundings to the futility of escape. As he looked about, he realized it was a strange place, an island small enough to see its entire perimeter from where he stood. It stretched little more than a kilometer in each direction, with a rocky beach around much of the island. Then nothing, nothing but water in every direction.

He felt no real fear, although a strange disquiet filled his being. He felt no hunger, longing, nor the many needs *of his former life. He felt only confusion about the past and a vague uncertainty about the future.*

His only compelling thoughts were: How did I get here? Why am I here? How did I come to such a fate? What is my destiny?

Moving almost without thinking, he began to make his way toward the only other living thing on "his island;" he already considered this place his own.

Of course he had seen the tree from atop the large rock, but it looked so natural that he had not consciously thought about it. Now it seemed not only to be important, but it seemed to draw him near.

The tree was large and imposing, and it dominated the landscape to his right.

"Perhaps at the tree I will find some answers," he said aloud, although there was no one to hear.

As he neared the tree, he felt more alive than any time since his wakening on the rock. As he drew closer, a sense of calm and enlightenment increased with every step. He was slowly overcoming his confusion and vague feelings of uncertainty as he approached the shade of the tree.

Then, as he crossed the shadow line of the tree, he knew that, if his destiny were to stay forever in the shade of this tree, he would be safe and content.

A magnificent tree, it appeared to be of faultless form. It was the most perfect tree he had ever seen or could imagine. Its long, flat, reed-like leaves were exquisite, each a replica of the other. Its bark seemed cleverly crafted and wonderfully strong.

Truly, this is a tree that will delight all who see it or rest in its shade, he thought.

The leaves of the tree seemed quite fragrant, and he noticed there was a strange fruit on the tree, almost hidden among the leaves. The fruit was red with streaks of yellow and orange, unlike anything he had ever seen. Feeling himself in need of nourishment, he plucked a piece of fruit and tried a small portion. Finding it quite tasty, he ate the whole fruit, and then another, and another.

It refreshed his body and greatly improved his feelings. At least I won't starve, he thought.

Sated now, he sat at the base of the tree and realized he was very tired. But the wind had suddenly turned quite cold, and he felt himself in need of shelter. Realizing the only possible warmth would be from the leaves of the tree, he picked several fallen leaves from the ground. Covering himself with the leaves, he found they were warm and inviting beyond anything he could have imagined.

He closed his eyes and drifted off to sleep.

He was unsure of how long he had slept or if he had dreamed, but when he awoke he was still on the island, still surrounded by the peacefulness of the tree.

Almost at the precise moment of his waking, when the calmness of the tree's shade seemed to once again invade his very soul, he sensed before he heard, heard before he saw, and knew without further thought, that he was not alone.

Out of the sky above he felt, heard, and saw a huge, magnificent brown–black bird descend into the upper branches.

At first, he was overwhelmed by curiosity, and then fear. Although he had never in his life seen such a bird, he knew what it was, and his growing sense of well-being vanished as quickly as it had come.

2. The Eagle

"We come here this day, not to mourn a death, but to celebrate a life.

"Robert Wayne Stone, who departed this life just two days ago, was known by many names.

"To his wife, he was known by special names only whispered between those who love and live together for so long.

"To his children, he was as much their friend as their father. They called him simply, but with love and affection, 'Dad.'

"To those who worked with him for so many years, he was known as Rob.

"But the name Rob came to mean so many things to so many people when it was used in reference to this fine individual.

"It meant living the courage of his convictions, particularly when it ran counter to prevailing wisdom.

"I grew up with him and worked beside him for nearly thirty years, often during times of great difficulty. In that whole time, I never heard a negative word from him about our problems or our future.

"To me, he epitomized the American values with which we were raised — values that now seem to be lost in the rush to face the competition from home and abroad.

"Rob had three priorities: God, his family, and his work. But they seemed for Rob to be but one.

"His work defined his whole being, was nourished by his religion, and enlivened by his family.

"Rob loved his country and was proud to call the Midwest home. He believed there was something magic in the soil, in the water, and in the air of the Midwest that created a special breed of people, with a sense of purpose and a strength of will found in few other places in the world."

With that, the speaker paused and turned his head away. He raised his hand to his now-hidden face and appeared to be wiping something from his eyes. Then, once again, he faced his audience. He breathed deeply. He glanced briefly over the seated crowd before him, then let his eyes return to the page and began once again to speak. This time his voice had a slight quiver.

"I was his co-worker, his friend, his brother. I will miss him.

"We will all miss his strength of character, his conviction, his sense of purpose, his certainty of right and wrong, his commitment, and his courage.

"He was an eagle."

With that, Ted Stone, younger brother of Rob, finished his eulogy and stepped from the pulpit.

Two days before, Robert Wayne Stone had succumbed, after a long and valiant fight against a hidden enemy—cancer—that had finally claimed his life.

He had died as he had lived, full of hope and determined to win.

Born to modest surroundings, his father a recent immigrant to the United States from Europe, Rob grew up in a family given to hard work and sacrifice.

His family moved several times as his father pursued increasingly illusive jobs during the so-called Great Depression. However, by the time he entered high school, Rob and his family had planted roots in central Wisconsin, in a town that Rob came quickly—and forever—to consider home.

An exceptional student and athlete, Rob lettered in both football and hockey. In the cold Wisconsin winters, his father, who knew little of the sport, nonetheless built an outdoor ice rink where Rob and Ted spent hours playing hockey with neighborhood kids. They lived close enough to the border that they were able to listen to radio broadcasts, *Hockey Night in Canada*, on Saturday nights. Rob, particularly, immersed himself on the intricacies of the game, envisioning the swift movements and deft play of his heroes.

Rob's hockey skills became so good that he was recruited to play hockey for the University of Minnesota. His hockey, which he loved so much, was about to pay for his schooling.

His third year of college was his best academically and on the ice. His studies were going very well, but he seemed to be in a groove with hockey. Rob made the Western Division All-Star team that year and was named a second team All-American.

Because of his high academic standing, he was also named to the Dean's List. His hockey buddies, many of whom had trouble staying on the team because of their academic standing, kidded him unmercifully about his academic performance and dubbed him the "Professor." He took the kidding in stride but regretted that his father, who had died the previous summer from a heart attack, was not around to share in the results of his hard work. Rob led the University of Minnesota team in goals and assists that year, and he was elected captain of the team for his senior year. But it was not to be.

During a game one Sunday afternoon in early December against the University of Michigan—a game they lost badly despite Rob's three goals—the announcers at the rink broadcast the news that the Japanese had attacked Pearl Harbor.

That spring, knowing he would get drafted eventually, Rob enlisted in the navy, although he could never remember being in a boat larger than his father's canoe.

Because of his advanced education, Rob went directly to officer candidate school and soon found himself actively engaged in the war effort. He expected to be shipped out to the Pacific, but was instead assigned to the Office of Naval Intelligence in Washington, where, for most of the next three years, he watched the progression of hostilities from a "war room."

At the university, he had added an Asian Studies minor to his engineering course of study, as he had always been fascinated by the "mysterious East." Consequently, he ended up on the Navy intelligence team concerned with China.

In the meantime his younger brother, Ted, just finishing high school, was drafted into the army and soon found himself slugging his way through the Pacific Islands, hitting most of the major battles with the Japanese, including Guadalcanal and Corregidor.

Rob repeatedly requested a transfer to join the fighting in the Pacific, but his exceptional abilities in his job kept him firmly rooted in D.C. Finally, as the hostilities were drawing to a close, his superiors granted him his wish, and he was on his way to the Pacific.

En route, the Japanese surrendered, and he ended up pushing paper at General MacArthur's headquarters in the Imperial Hotel in Tokyo.

He spent nearly two years with the U.S. occupation

forces in Tokyo and twice went to China with a team trying to negotiate the release of Japanese prisoners held by the Chinese and Russians.

Once, while on leave, he was able to travel to Kyoto, the fabled historic and cultural capital of Japan. While there, he heard that the Chinese had released some Japanese prisoners-of-war, who were then making their way through Korea and who were to be transferred on the USS *Cherokee* back to Japan.

Rushing back to Tokyo, he requested permission to join the *Cherokee* for her mission. It would be as close as he ever got to a Japanese fighting soldier — real soldiers from the war that he seemed to have missed.

Although a short journey back to Japan from the Korean Peninsula, many of the Japanese soldiers aboard the *Cherokee* had great difficulty with the trip. They were sick, undernourished, and feeble from their captivity and long march. He had only one brief encounter with a ragged but determined-looking Japanese soldier, with whom he shared a cigarette and a laugh on the deck of the *Cherokee*.

This soldier's uniform, like the rest of their number, was so ragged that it was nearly impossible to tell his rank. However, Rob sensed that he was an officer because of the silent respect and deference shown him by the other Japanese soldiers as they passed.

Unable to communicate, they spent their few moments together enjoying the cigarettes and mist that was then enveloping the ship. Preoccupied with his duties, Rob never saw the soldier again during the short trip.

His military time soon up, he returned to the U.S. for a brief visit with his family. Going back to college for his final year, he switched his major from civil to mechanical engineering and graduated high in his class. He accepted a position with the world's leading producer of farm equipment, based in Indiana. He headed there almost directly from school, stopping in his hometown only long enough to marry his high school sweetheart.

Beginning his training with the engineering design group, he rotated over a three-year period through all the important engineering and manufacturing departments of the company. While he enjoyed his work, he longed to return to his home in Wisconsin.

One evening during his third summer in Indiana, his brother called. Ted was now a production worker at the heavy-earth moving equipment plant in his hometown. Rob and Ted had always been close, despite the fact that they had been apart for some ten years. His brother had not gone on to college, instead going to work in a plant directly upon his return from the war. It was the very same plant that had brought their father to town more than twenty-five years earlier.

Ted's call was to tell Rob that the plant, a supply facility to the mother plant in Kansas, was expanding rapidly and was looking for someone to start up a new engineering department. Rob would be perfect he said, and of course the family, both Ted and their father, had excellent work records at the plant.

Soon Rob was back in his hometown and heading up the new engineering department. He relished his new job, and his young family flourished and grew, first with a son and then a daughter. Rob junior resembled his father and over the years, followed in his footsteps in many ways.

Although not quite as good a student, to Rob's delight his son eventually wore his father's number on the high school hockey team. Rob even accepted gracefully the fact that his son broke his scoring record in only his sophomore year. Rob felt his son was the first genuine professional hockey prospect ever from their hometown.

For many years the work at the plant grew in volume and diversity as the company opened new markets both at home and abroad.

Then, near the end of the late sixties, the company encountered increasing competition and began to lose a few customers here and there. They still held a commanding position in their field, however, and management was able to keep profits growing by increasing the prices they charged for their products.

Everyone in the company knew they would face more and more competition, but they all believed it would be from low-wage countries, offering a cheaper but inferior product.

The company response was to encourage workers to work harder and even to adopt some of the techniques, like quality circles, that the Americans themselves had taught the Japanese. But as Rob pointed out to Ted on more than one occasion, the plant was very old and didn't lend itself easily to many of these techniques.

Over the next two decades, the competition, particularly from Japan, grew tougher and tougher. The Japanese kept their prices low but seemed to increase quality and introduce new products at an alarming speed.

Rob was an innovator and, over time, was able to talk management into introducing a whole series of new methods to improve plant production. On several occasions, however, some of these methods ran afoul of the union, and Rob and Ted, now a union leader at the plant, found themselves at odds.

At such times, work relations between the two became strained, but they tried hard never to let it interfere with family gatherings.

One time, however, all the pent-up frustrations on both sides boiled over. Rob had been reading about self-directed work teams as an aid to quality improvement and worker productivity. He wanted to try some experimental teams in the plant but insisted that specific productivity goals were necessary. The union took the position that the goals were too difficult and would result either in the loss of jobs or wage rate and job classification losses.

The controversy pitted the two brothers against each other in public, with both feeling obligated not to budge because any backing down would appear to be a concession for family reasons. In private, their relations, although strained, remained cordial. However, it wasn't until years after the plant closed that they really forgave each other.

Ted was highly regarded by the union rank and file, and he eventually rose to be the full-time union representative, working exclusively on union matters at the plant and at several other local manufacturing sites where the union represented the production workers.

For his part, Rob was eventually appointed assistant plant manager, then plant manager. The company asked him to become the general manager of the division at the headquarters in Kansas, but Rob declined, preferring to stay in his hometown.

The decision was a tough one for the family. It would have meant the recognition of all Rob's hard work and a chance to try out the new ideas he had been working on to restructure and refocus his division. But personal events intervened.

Rob's son had gone on to college, graduated, married his high school sweetheart, and was living in Dallas. He and his wife were expecting their second child by their third year there. That spring, on the way home to visit his family in Wisconsin, he was killed in a car accident. His wife and son, injured only slightly, survived. They came to live with Rob for awhile, then settled in a house around the corner.

Rob was both grandfather and father to the boy and the young daughter who was born six months after the accident. He had his grandson on skates almost before he could walk. He even coached his teams through his tenth birthday, when things at work began to seriously deteriorate.

After the death of his son, Rob buried his grief in his work. Reaching a new partnership with the union, Rob initiated many new programs in the areas of quality, productivity, product line consolidation, work flow, and supplier relations. But despite all his hard work, by the late eighties competition was so intense that company management at the headquarters—young, financially oriented people brought in to turn the company around —began to lay off large numbers of workers.

One of the major casualties was the plant in Wisconsin, as management decided to close it and open a new facility just across the U.S. border in Mexico.

Rob's brother, Ted, unable to find work in his hometown, moved his family to Milwaukee, where he was able to find a maintenance job in one of the city's famous breweries.

Rob, however, found a job within a few months as a salesman for a manufacturing firm selling robotics equipment to the burgeoning electronics industry. Rob had never in his life sold anything, and he found the transition a difficult one. With only a few years to go before retirement, he was determined to make the best of it. He found the "cold calls" the hardest but enjoyed working with plant engineers once a sale was made.

However, he disliked the travel intensely, as he was

often on the road all week. He missed his family and, in particular, regretted not being there for his grandson's hockey games.

Rob worked hard to meet his sales quotas, and over the six years with the company, he only missed it twice. When he did make his quota, it was just barely. It was with some relief that he took an early retirement package—although it was not very lucrative—and settled into this new phase of his life.

Unfortunately, it was shortly after his retirement that Rob, complaining of recurring pain, discovered that he had pancreatic cancer.

✵ ✵ ✵

He was in better physical condition than the average man his age, he thought, but his arms now felt leaden and no longer up to the task. Bone weary, they had never before worked in such a monotonous, repetitive way. They were about to give out.

With that thought he looked down and was startled to see he was in the air. Alone! Flying!

Flying horizontal to the ground at a frightening height, he realized that his arms were not arms at all, but wings. Large, majestic wings of brown-black feathers tipped in white.

"But I can't fly," he thought, and with that he began to fall—slowly at first, looping around in circles, then diving directly, headlong toward the water.

The water rushed toward him at a terrifying speed.

With less than a hundred yards between him and

impending doom, he knew he would never survive the crash at this speed.

It was then he saw the island. It seemed almost to stop him in midair.

"Maybe if I flap my arms—my wings—hard enough," he said to himself, *"I could make it to that island."*

As he began to slow his descent and to level out just above the breaking water, he felt the breeze and knew that this breeze was a mixed blessing. It gave him some lift upon which to soar, but he also knew that this was a breeze that contained the potential for a storm—a terrible storm against which he would eventually have to struggle.

He began to flap, uncoordinated at first but then in graceful, smooth arcs, powerfully propelling himself skyward.

He soon gained some altitude and, with that altitude, a growing confidence that he could reach the island.

As the island loomed closer, he felt he could now afford a quick look at the rest of his body. But first he stole another glance at those wings, almost frightening in their span and beauty.

He was only mildly surprised to see that the rest of the body matched the wings. Sleek, robust, aerodynamic and covered in feathers, much the same as the wings—shiny, brown-black and tipped in a snowy white.

"I am an eagle!" he cried.

"Eagles can fly," he knew, and with that revelation, the tiredness left his wings.

The island no longer seemed so far away, and he began to feel that he could fly forever.

He now realized he didn't need the island, so he headed skyward and began long, circling trails through the sky and clouds. He soared freely and with a growing sense of exhilaration. He felt his strength actually increase as he flew higher—quite opposite of how, at first, he thought it would work.

It was a powerful feeling, almost intoxicating. He could see for miles in every direction and move at lightning speed—up, down, left, right.

Let it never end, this feeling of freedom, control, and certainty of purpose, this all-seeing, all-being moment, he thought. He flew for hours until he sighted land, a land that looked vaguely familiar, but he could not place it. He flew across the land for many miles, looking at the fields and small villages. Soon he was over a large city that was quite strange to him with its mix of modern buildings and many wide streets and with its hundreds of large wooden structures, many surrounded by beautiful gardens.

One such structure attracted his attention, and he circled it several times, watching with curiosity the people coming and going in small groups. He cast a large shadow over one old woman who was struggling up the stairs to the building, as he came between her and the sun. He felt an overwhelming sense of connection with the old woman but also a strange and unsettling feeling of intrusion into her life. He turned quickly skyward and flew back toward the sea.

Again he flew for many hours across the villages and back to the sea, unsure of where he was heading—or why. He flew for many hours.

It was then he saw the island once again.

It drew him toward it like the Sirens in some Greek myth. He had little power to resist. Slowly he gained altitude and turned to the left to approach with the wind in his face. He flew toward the island with conviction but without choice.

"Where will a mighty eagle land on such a rocky barren island?" he asked himself.

And then he saw the tree—a tree of such grandeur and perfection that it was truly a fitting place for an eagle as powerful as him to land.

As he swept down toward the tree, he noticed a monk sitting in the shade of the tree. He knew that before this frightening wind, full of foreboding, he would have to deal with this monk.

Before his talons even gripped the branch high in the tree, he was wondering how this monk came to be here. He knew instinctively that this monk did not think like him, that he came from another tradition, and that he surely would not have the beliefs of an eagle.

More importantly, even though he was sure he could never have seen him before, a small, nagging, sense of familiarity tugged at his thoughts. One thing was for sure, though; he knew that the monk was a decisive force in bringing him to this place.

3. The Rock

"Eagle!" called the monk, as he looked skyward through the branches of the tree. "What brings you to my island?"

Shielding his eyes from the sun, the monk could barely make out the shape of the giant bird perched high in the tree.

The eagle seemed either to ignore or to disdain the monk. The eagle made no sound but gazed out to sea.

"Eagle," the monk said again, "hear my words. I need to know, what brings you to my island?"

"Who put *you* in charge of this island?" demanded the eagle.

The question seemed to encircle and descend upon the monk as if it were a heavy rain.

"Neither title nor status do I seek or hold," the monk responded after a short reflection. "I am but a simple monk. I am ashamed that you thought I was suggesting some worth beyond my station. In my tradition, we say, 'the nail that sticks out gets hammered down.'

"In charge of this island? Never," said the monk humbly, his eyes now looking at the ground.

"I would need many years to understand such a role. And then many more to correct my numerous defects.

"You must understand, eagle, I do not claim to dominate my environment—no person can do so. Although I do not know how long I have been here, I call it *my* island because I am part of it, and it of me.

"Neither could be master of the other," the monk continued, now looking up once again at the eagle. "We are one."

"That cannot be so," said the eagle, the words now like a laser beam targeting the monk.

"Human nature commands that there are those who lead and those who follow. There is a natural hierarchy— a natural order of things that ordain the worth of each based on their accomplishments, their status in society, and the things they possess. Someone must be in charge—must be the leader," cried the eagle. "If you do not claim it, I will."

"So be it," said the monk. "You be the leader if you think you can!"

"So I shall, for I can see for many miles from my lofty perch, and can fly in any direction I choose. You cannot do these things, monk."

With that the monk acknowledged the powers of the eagle, but was reluctant to speak of the many things he himself had done, or could do. He thought instead of the growing belief that he had met this eagle before, although he knew it could not be so.

"What are you staring at, monk?" demanded the eagle. "Your eyes betray your soul, and your soul is troubled. Is it because I am now in charge?"

"You are wise, eagle, and you know my heart. I am troubled. Troubled by many things."

"Speak, monk, for it is my role as leader to care for your troubles. What bothers you so much?"

The monk looked down at his sandals, as he did not wish to see the eagle as he spoke.

"In another life I have known much danger and hardship. And I was afraid, many, many times. I faced starvation and such depravations that I have never allowed myself to think of them again. I once had a hand so fine that I could create wonderful calligraphy, and then, it was damaged beyond repair. It was the most grievous event of my life.

"And I have seen many die, and have been close to dying myself. I saw so much tragedy that I put aside my self-pity and focused only on living.

"And I was richly rewarded. First with survival and then with a productive life. At times I have considered myself to be among the most fortunate of men — rich, not with wealth, but with the respect of those with whom I worked, and with a fine strong family.

"I could, and did, face all of life's challenges with a steady face." He was looking up now at the eagle, "but now I am facing my greatest challenge."

The monk paused briefly, then continued: "I am not sure of how I got here or even if I am a monk. I have changed; I am away from everything I know and hold dear. And, I am afraid of this change."

The eagle looked to the sky, unsure of how to respond. Should he speak of his own fears, of the changes that he, as well, did not understand?

It seemed that many minutes had passed when the monk finally broke the silence.

"You must think me unworthy, eagle, as you have not responded to me."

"No, monk, I do not think you unworthy. But I *do* believe you are a monk. From my vantage point I can see very far, as I told you, but my experiences have also helped me see deep within the soul as well. You are a monk, very much a monk, and you have always been so, despite your many outward guises.

"That is why I think I can speak to you now. For it is not in the nature of eagles to be open, to speak what is in their hearts. We are to be brave, to fight against that which frightens us. I feel somehow that we have a connection, from somewhere deep in our past, from somewhere I can't remember.

"But more importantly, I sense a connection of our spirits, of our aspirations, and of our lives. Even though we come from very different traditions, you and I, I think we are the same in many ways. And so, monk, I will tell you my heart."

He paused, then began again to speak, this time almost in a whisper. "Your fears, it seems, are not yours alone," confided the eagle, "for I face them myself. I am not sure how long I've been an eagle, although I have no doubt that I am one now.

"How I came to be one, though, and how I came to this island is a great mystery to me. And what I don't understand frightens me more than any physical fear I have ever known."

"It seems we share more than the common fate of this island," said the monk. "Can we sit side by side and speak of this as equals?"

"Yes," responded the eagle, "perhaps we could sit together on that rock. It has a view that can be shared by us both."

"I agree. It is a fine, high rock with a perfect view of our surroundings. I always like to get a perspective when I talk of weighty matters."

The eagle flew to the rock, and the monk followed quickly behind. They sat on the rock together as each in turn spoke the story of his life and its many challenges.

Each had faced many obstacles and had many opportunities. They talked many hours, continuing without stop throughout the day and into the late afternoon.

They discovered that their lives were, in many ways, a series of changes—constant, relentless, and inevitable. They agreed near evening that change was perhaps the only constant in their lives.

As much as the changes themselves, they talked of how they faced the changes and their attitudes to the changes at various times in their lives.

The monk spoke of his captivity and the loss of his ability to practice his sacred and much-loved calligraphy. In hushed tones, he spoke of his regrets that the pressures of his work kept him so often from his family.

The eagle spoke of his losses: his father and his son, the devastation of the plant closing, and the difficulty of learning so many new skills near the end of his career. He spoke also of the cancer that had ravaged his earthly body.

"With so many challenges, such changes are unfair," said the monk, and the eagle nodded his head in agreement.

After many hours of talking, they came to understand that their acceptance of change was, perhaps, the greatest predictor of how they handled change.

At last, they talked of their greatest change, their arrival on the island. Each now knew how, but not why, he had come to be here.

"I understand now that I was not alone, nor am I alone here, in my fear of change," said the monk.

"Perhaps our only choice is to embrace change, to make it part of us," added the eagle as he looked out to sea for a long time.

"I am tired," said the eagle finally, "from my long flight, and from our talk. I must sleep. Despite the serenity of this rock, I would feel safer in the tree."

"I have slept beneath the tree and feel comfortable there as well," replied the monk. "I will sleep under the warmth of its leaves."

It had grown dark as they spoke, and the eagle, despite his excellent eye sight, did not notice a strange object glowing in the water amidst the growing dusk of the evening.

The wind had begun to pick up, and water now swirled onto the shore. From amongst the whitecaps of the water surrounding the island, a large head emerged unseen from the depths, and two piercing green eyes silently watched the eagle and the monk as they left the rock and made their way toward the tree.

4. The Island

"Wake up, monk!" shouted the eagle. "I have been awake for some time."

"Good morning, eagle."

The monk rose from the base of the tree where he had slept and looked at the sky, then back to the high branches of the tree where the eagle had nested for the night. He stretched as he felt the warmth of the sun and the freshness of the morning air.

"I trust you slept well in your lofty perch, eagle?

"It seems we have another fine day. Perhaps

we could go to that small beach on the far side and enjoy the sun for awhile."

"There is not time for that now, monk; there are some important things we need to discuss."

"Speak then, eagle, for you sound very serious."

"I am, monk. I have enjoyed our short time together, and I learned much from our talk as we sat on the rock yesterday. But I must leave soon, and I want to say good-bye."

The monk stared up at the eagle in silence, as he was saddened by the loss of his new friend so soon after they had met, and by the fact that he would once again be alone on this island.

"Before I go, I wanted to talk to you," the eagle continued. "I fear for your safety."

"As I told you yesterday, eagle, I have little concern for my physical well-being, and I now fear only the uncertainty of why I'm here. What is my destiny to be? I'm afraid that if I stay alone on this island, my life will have little purpose. The lack of any real meaning for my life is what I fear most."

"I understand this well, monk, for it is the reason I must go. I know little of why I am here, or why I'm on this island talking to you. No disrespect meant.

"But I do know that I am an eagle, and eagles fly. So that is what I must do. Fly. I plan to leave as soon as I've eaten. Have you found anything to eat on the island?"

"Yes," said the monk, "the fruit of this tree is quite tasty, and filling too."

"Is it safe?" asked the eagle. "It doesn't look like any fruit I have seen before."

"I'm alive," said the monk, "as you can see. I ate several pieces yesterday, and I'm still here. It is as perfect a food as I have ever tasted."

"They all look so good," said the eagle. "How do we know which are ripe?"

"The fruit falls when it is ripe," said the monk.

With that, the eagle flew to the ground in order to eat the ripest fruit, while the monk moved to some fruit lying on the ground near the shade line.

They both ate several pieces of fruit and agreed that it was excellent, better than anything either had ever eaten.

"Well," said the eagle, "the fruit is good, as you promised. It is as perfect as the rest of the tree." With that, he flew back to the high center branches of the tree.

The monk twisted his neck to better see the eagle, now largely obscured by the dense leaves near the interior of the tree.

"I believe this tree could teach us many things as well as offering us food and shelter, eagle," said the monk, moving closer to the tree so he could again see the eagle as he spoke.

"I agree it is a fine tree, monk, and I think you are right about what it might teach us, but we have more serious things to discuss, as I told you.

"I can see very far from this tree, and while the sun shines brightly now, I can see troublesome clouds in the distance," the eagle said as he looked to his left. "Since we have been awake, they have moved much closer. Can you feel the increasing strength of the wind?

"I think you should leave, too, monk, and soon. My eagle sense tells me that this storm carries much danger."

"An eagle as wise as yourself should know that I cannot leave this island," replied the monk. "There is no way for me to do so. There is no boat and no way to build one. And while I feel quite young in spirit, my body is old and unable to swim very far. Besides, in which direction would I swim?"

"You must try something," pleaded the eagle. "I am warning you, you cannot stay here much longer."

"Thank you for your concern, eagle, but I will stay and await my fate, for I am alone."

"Yesterday before I came to this island, I flew in many directions, and I saw no land." The eagle paused to think. "I would carry you if I could, monk, but I know I could not do so for very long. "Perhaps, if I leave soon, I may be able to find land or some help. But I do not think I have much time. The storm is approaching quickly. You must try to do something."

"I accept the fact that I can do little or nothing on my own— nor could any person or any thing in this situation," said the monk, as he twisted again so his eyes could see the bird more clearly. "Without the help of others, I am lost. I will accept my fate gracefully."

"No! No! You must think of something," cried the eagle, growing increasingly agitated at the monk's lack of concern. "Think. Use your natural creativity to find some means of escape!"

"Escape. I could not, nor could anyone, undertake and succeed at such an enterprise alone. I would need much help. This is not just an old monk's belief; this is the true law of nature."

As he spoke, the wind, which had been blowing harder by the minute, began to pick up the leaves around the base of the tree and swirl them around at the monk's feet.

"For example," explained the monk, "this tree, so perfect in its shape and in each detail, is the product of many things—the seed that gave it birth, the earth that gave it a home, the rain that fed its growth, the sun that nourished its leaves, even the clouds that gave it occasional shelter. Each of these elements of nature made a meaningful contribution to the final result. Even this wind helped the tree to be strong but flexible."

Mention of the wind caused him to pause and to quietly contemplate the future.

The wind may have helped the tree, but both the eagle and the monk knew in his own way that this was now a wind that meant change for them both.

The eagle had listened intently as the monk spoke. Breaking finally from his silent thoughts, he acknowledged the monk's words.

"You are right about this thing, monk. This truly is a beautiful tree—perfect in every detail. It needed the unique contribution of the soil, sun and water to make

it what it is. Each has had its role and contributed to the
result. This tree now offers me a perch and you shade."

The eagle glanced in the direction of the storm and
knew the time to leave was at hand. Discussing such
things was important, he knew, but not at such times.
Didn't this monk know the dangers? While the time is
short, I will try one more time, quickly, to reason with
him, he thought, but then I must leave.

The eagle spoke rapidly and with conviction, hoping
his words would move the monk. "But this tree would
not exist without a strong individual seed.

"The seed that started this tree may not have been the
most perfect or powerful of all seeds. But this seed had
an obligation to be its best—to achieve its destiny even
if the wind or rain or sun or soil was not the best."

They looked away from each other as if to steal a few
moments of private thought. Each recognized that the
other had made his case succinctly and well.

Just then, a powerful rush of wind intruded rudely
into their thoughts by breaking several of the tree's
larger branches.

One of the largest fell directly on the eagle and
knocked him sprawling to the ground at the feet of the
monk.

5. The Wind

When he finally awoke, he realized he was in the arms of the monk and it bothered the eagle greatly.

"Let me go, monk," he said defiantly. "Do not hold me like this!"

"You're hurt badly, and you need help," responded the monk.

With that the eagle felt the sharp pain in his wing. It began to throb constantly as he slowly regained consciousness.

"How did this happen?" the eagle asked aggressively, trying to hide his pain.

"The wind sprang up suddenly and ferociously, and it broke some large branches from the tree. One of them hit you from behind and knocked you to the ground," said the monk. "The branches just missed me by inches."

"This wind seems to be a curse," said the eagle, now content to rest a short time longer in the arms of the monk. "Do you know where it gets its power?"

"I have been thinking about this wind since I came here to this island," sighed the monk. "I believe this wind is the breath of a billion people. It will be an unrelenting challenge for many years."

"You are right. I have the same uneasiness about this wind. I believe we will need to rethink our beliefs about each other and even about our own people," said the eagle, "if we are to learn to deal with such a wind." Again, sensing his vulnerability in the arms of the monk, he said, "Now, set me down!"

"But you need help," said the monk. "Trust me in this."

"I want to trust you," the eagle said, his yellow eyes now focused directly at the monk, "but I do not know if I can. I have been taught that you can trust only yourself and few others."

As the eagle spoke, the monk was admiring many things about the eagle. For centuries he had represented power, might, dominion, and conquest—but also, to the monk the eagle represented the vital spiritual link between heaven and earth. This eagle is so powerful he could carry souls to heaven! What power he could have if he could but trust! thought the monk.

"Why do you look at me so?" cried the eagle in a voice that seemed more like a high-pitched scream.

"For an eagle, trust is a very difficult matter. It is not something you can give. Trust is something one must earn."

The eagle looked at the monk with a penetrating stare that seemed to pierce right to the soul of the monk. "I cannot trust someone who has not proven himself to me. To really trust you, I would need to know you for a long time and see how you react to and deal with many different situations," explained the eagle. "Trust is conditional and changes with the circumstances. To me trust is proven in very specific and tangible ways. It is the way of the eagle."

"This is quite different from my idea of trust," the monk responded. "Quite different!"

"In what ways?" questioned the eagle. "As an eagle I trust above all my ability to learn new things, to constantly challenge tradition. So I am eager to hear your concept of trust. Speak! Speak! But first, put me down!"

By this time, the monk was glad to do so. This eagle is heavy, he thought. He must weigh more than fifty pounds, a lot to hold for a monk of my age. Setting the eagle gently to the ground, the monk then settled himself on the ground near the eagle.

The wind was blowing even more strongly now, bending the tree limbs and creating thousands of whitecaps on the surface of the water surrounding the island. It contained the seeds of an impending storm, and both the eagle and the monk were keenly aware of its growing strength.

The monk looked first to the sky, then back to the eagle.

"For monks, trust is not a complicated thing, although to an eagle it may seem so. In many ways, trust is life itself," he said. "Those who trust the most are in turn the most trusted. I can trust all other monks from my group, even if I have never before met them. I know they believe as I do, share the same values, honor the same traditions, follow the same rules, and revere the same institutions.

"Within our groups, trust is given implicitly and freely. I do not trust newness for the sake of newness but trust tradition and the wisdom of my ancestors. I do not trust my own decisions but trust in the collective wisdom of all monks. I trust the . . ."

"Hold it, monk," interrupted the eagle. "These things in which you trust may have been worthwhile in times past, but will they help you face the power of the wind which now assaults our island?"

The monk recognized that the eagle spoke the truth, that the power of the wind could change many of the things he believed in and held sacred. He looked deeply into the eyes of the eagle, who was wincing with pain, although he seemed to go to great lengths not to let it show.

For the next few moments they sat silently listening to the rising sea pounding the rocks. The silence felt natural to the monk, but it bothered the eagle. The eagle felt every moment had merit and should not be wasted. He did not like to squander even one minute, and quiet meditation seemed like a great waste. He stared at the monk, almost willing him to speak.

The monk returned the eagle's stare and thought that the eagle's gleaming white head, with its pronounced brow, penetrating eyes, and poised alertness, spoke without words of the eagle's courage, determination, and fortitude.

Finally, in frustration and pain, the eagle cried, "Enough of this, monk! No more silence and no more talk either. We must do something! I really do not need to trust you, monk, if you'll do what I say. We'll make a pact, a contract," argued the eagle. "It's the only way for us to work together."

The monk had never been a party to a pact, or any such contract for that matter. He had always trusted those with whom he worked. An agreement among monks would always be honored, in the event of the unexpected, or even natural disasters! An agreement was a sacred trust, and virtually nothing could relieve him of his obligations.

"With this wind picking up strongly, time is too short to talk of contracts," said the monk. "But there is one more thing I must tell you, and it is difficult, very difficult, for me to do so, eagle," he said quietly.

"Forget the contract. Speak. Speak," replied the eagle loudly.

"I hesitate to speak of this, eagle, because it is very painful for me. You see, I am not sure how well I can use my right hand. I will need two hands to fix your wing. This hand," said the monk holding out his right hand, which he had kept hidden in his robe, "was badly damaged many years ago, and I have never used it since. It may not work for me now."

The eagle briefly studied the right hand of the monk, now clearly visible to him. He looked into the eyes of the monk. "I believe in you, monk. I have to. Now, get busy and fix my wing so that I can fly once again!"

"I will try my best. Please trust me," pleaded the monk.

"Enough! Enough! Fix the wing!" screeched the eagle, now willing to show his considerable pain.

With that the monk reached for the broken wing. At first, the eagle recoiled but only slightly so. He then surrendered himself completely to the monk.

Quickly, but gently, the monk took the wing into his hands. Surprisingly, although clumsily, his right hand responded as he had hoped. Feeling for the break, the monk slid his hands on either side of the powerful bone now separated by the break. The right hand held the upper portion of the bone in place. With the left, he gave a deft twist, snapping the two pieces into alignment. He felt the eagle flinch. But it was over. The eagle appeared to regain the fire in his eyes almost immediately, and he held his head a little higher than before.

The monk smiled broadly. "When I held your wing, I felt your power—the power of the individual. I have always held myself back in deference to others. I could not assert my own strength without losing face. And it is the first time I have used my right hand, since . . . since . . ." The monk hesitated. "I must resist any more thoughts of this. It is dangerous for a monk to think of his own importance . . ."

A strange sensation stopped the monk, and the eagle felt it, too. It was as if someone, or something, was watching them.

With that the eagle took flight, and despite his recently broken wing, he was able to fly to the top of the tree, very near where he had perched when he first arrived on the island. He struck a gallant pose, with his proud head thrust high into the air against the wind, his wings spread widely, his talons tightly clutching a spray of branches.

The monk turned and sat at the base of the tree, chanting silently to himself.

The eagle and the monk realized, each in his own way, that this island, to which they had both come so mysteriously, was a special place. They knew instinctively that this island was a place of great learning, a place where the unusual is usual, where the unexpected is expected, and where the extraordinary is ordinary.

Soon the wind began to howl and the eagle rejoined the monk at the base of the tree, not wanting to take the chance of another injury. However, the wind became so loud that the eagle and the monk could hardly hear one another as they talked. The wind became almost gale-force in strength, but the worst was the sound. It thundered and rumbled until it was the only sound to be heard. Even the tree, for all its majesty, began to bend and creak. Shifting closer together, the eagle and the monk tried their best to shout over the now-deafening noise.

Just as dusk was beginning to fall, the same strange glowing eyes emerged from the water as they had the night before. This time, though, they were joined by many, many more pairs of large, green, almost translucent eyes, moving slowly toward the island and the eagle and the monk who sat huddled against the wind.

6. The Nest

Both the monk and the eagle slept fitfully that night, each awake at times when the wind was loudest. They never spoke during those periods of sleeplessness but lay silently in nervous anticipation of events to come. Finally, near dawn, both slept soundly as they succumbed to nervous exhaustion.

The next morning as he arose, this time even before the eagle had stirred, the monk stood and looked around at the rising water. It had risen enough to completely cover the small beach and submerge many of the rocks beyond that.

"Perhaps we *should* consider building a nest," suggested the monk, as he gently nudged the eagle awake, "although I have no desire to stay in this tree despite its beauty and perfection." He was watching with growing concern as the wind was causing the tree to bend deeply every few minutes. "But, frankly, I wouldn't know where to start, or what to do!"

"Well, nests come naturally to me, monk, although I'll be frank with you. I've never tried to build a nest large enough for a monk. For eagles, nests are our own personal space. We like to be alone in them, and we don't want a lot of company! Of course, the bigger the nest, the more important the eagle. But one big enough for a monk? Unheard of!" said the eagle.

But the monk disagreed. "Such a nest would not have to be large, eagle. Monks are quite accustomed to getting by with little space."

With that, the monk began to circle and collect the fallen branches of the tree, almost as if in defiance of what the eagle had said.

"Besides, we could build such a nest together, eagle!" suggested the monk.

Before the eagle could respond, the wind once again intruded on their discussion and caused them both to jump as more branches were ripped from the tree.

They ceased their talk as the wind began to consume their thoughts. Like a wind laden with rain, it seemed heavy with change. They could feel the change—like they could feel the coming rain—without seeing, but with a sense of knowing.

Despite their foreboding, they each felt enlightened and encouraged by a sense of knowing at least this one thing—that change was on the way. Despite their fear of change, it was in a strange way reassuring to know that change was coming. Better to know and prepare than to be caught unaware.

They held their heads high to drink in the wind, to breathe deeply of it. It was as if to say: "Come on, wind! We can deal with you!" Rather than defeat them, the wind energized them and made them bold.

The eagle turned to face the monk, disregarding the power of the wind. "We will work as a team, monk. Although I have always built my nest by myself, I think it is time I learned to work with you. This wind is threatening, and we need to get started."

"Thank you, eagle. I look forward to our work together. I ask only that we do not build the nest too high in this magnificent tree. Despite its obvious strength, I don't wish to be up too high with the strength of this wind. You can fly, but all I can do is pray!" laughed the monk.

"Good point, monk. We eagles normally look for the highest, most remote spots for our nests. For this nest, though, let's use this huge lower limb that forms a large cradle with the trunk. It will be large enough and strong enough. However, I think our biggest problem will be time. A nest large enough for an eagle and a monk will take forever to build!"

"Not if we work together as a team," explained the

monk, "because together we can do things that an individual could only dream of doing alone. The synergy of individual strengths coupled with like-minded others is the special magic of a team. Hard to explain, beautiful to watch!"

"We eagles have heard of the power of you monks and your teams. In fact, we eagles have begun to use some of your methods. We do so most often when we have to face a crisis. Then we assemble the best-performing eagles together in a group, particularly those who have demonstrated their strength individually."

Without seeming to notice or comment that they were working together, the eagle began to gather and stack the fallen branches.

"And how have they worked?" asked the monk, handing branch after branch to the eagle. As each branch was handed to him, the eagle skillfully fit it into place.

"As well as can be expected," responded the eagle. "These groups do well enough when called upon to do a specific task. But they're still quite limited, and they need a lot of supervision and control. You see, monk, my tradition—the cult of the eagle—dictates that individuals make the difference as we discussed earlier."

"Just like this tree . . ."

The monk dropped a large branch he was struggling with, interrupted the eagle, and argued. "But it was the many different elements of nature working together that had the power to create and shape the tree, not the tree itself. It is the 'team of nature' that has the power to change the tree, not the tree itself," he argued.

"In the case of the tree, its strength surely originates from its own unique, individual seed, but it's enhanced and enriched by the synergy of the team that surrounds it—the forces of nature, each playing a role," the eagle continued.

"We must celebrate both the individual and the group," added the monk, "if we are to survive and succeed in a time of challenge and change."

"Again, we are wasting too much time talking, monk! I decide quickly, while you like to talk and get agreement. I've already decided that I like this idea of teamwork, so let's work now and finish this nest. These strong leaves work well to hold the branches together," explained the eagle. "We need just a few more branches and some large leaves to complete the nest."

"I'll gather those large branches that hit you," said the monk, "if you can harvest those leaves high up in the tree."

With that, they began their final tasks in building the nest, each contributing in his own unique way—the eagle as the master architect, the monk encouraging him to new levels of achievement.

While finishing the last of the nest, the wind had given them a brief reprieve from its constant blowing. They had just completed the nest and were beginning to climb into it when the tree shook violently. They tumbled into the nest on top of one another and scrambled to right themselves.

It felt like an earthquake, but they both knew instinctively that it was the wind. Gale-force and unrelenting now, it forced the tree to bend and groan in defense.

"This is the best nest I've ever seen, monk, but even it will not stand up long to such a wind!" said the eagle. "Soon, even it won't be enough to protect us."

If they could have seen the movement in the waters behind them, they would have been worried about more than the nest.

7. The Sage

The tree shook violently for several minutes. The monk thought surely that the nest would be torn away from the tree. But then there was calm, and it seemed to settle back into the fork of the tree. Just as he allowed himself to relax, he felt himself falling, as the wind roared once again and the nest toppled from the tree.

Fortunately, his robe caught one of the lowest branches of the tree, breaking his fall just above the ground. It held him scarcely a moment, but it was enough to save him from serious injury. As it was, he landed on his side and was sure he had no broken bones or serious sprains.

The eagle fared much better, as he was able to take flight as the nest slipped from the tree. He landed seconds later near the monk.

The monk actually smiled as the eagle cautiously called out to him. Relieved to see the smile, the eagle raised his wings as if in salute but more in celebration — and relief.

"It is truly a powerful wind that can destroy such a nest," said the eagle, looking around him at the scattered remains of the nest. "I am sorry that it failed."

"There was no failure in this, eagle. We did our best," said the monk. "Besides, I am fine. I suffered no injuries. We must not waste time worrying about the nest. Instead, we should try again to build a shelter from this wind," said the monk in a voice that could barely be heard. "We must protect ourselves from this force that threatens to destroy us and our island. I believe our best protection would be a wall!"

"There is no wall that can long withstand this wind. We'd be better off building a raft and trying to sail away from here!" the eagle shouted back, his piercing voice attempting to penetrate through the sound of the wind.

"We have wood but little else to build a raft, so we must try to build a wall," shouted the monk in turn, "or else we'll die. Surely this is not our fate. We must live to tell others of our journey to this island and of the things we have learned about each other."

With that, the monk struggled to his feet and, leaning into the wind, surveyed the rocky landscape of the island. The island was not large, and it sloped sharply downward toward the sea.

Less than a hundred yards to the left of the tree, near the edge of the advancing water, he noticed a place where the rocks seemed to dip slightly into a crevice. There appeared to be enough room for two, and he thought, if I can put several larger rocks around the edge, perhaps that will form a protective wall.

He told the eagle of his plan and then, struggling against the wind, made his way slowly toward the crevice.

"You monks are more creative than I ever thought," said the eagle, leaning into the gale as he followed the monk.

"This looks like a good rock to start our wall," said the monk, and he bent to his task. The chosen rock would not budge, however, as it had a weight several times that of the monk. The monk straightened his body, inhaled deeply, then bent again to his task. Again, the rock resisted.

A second time the monk stood and tried to summon his strength. Again, he bent to the rock, almost willing both his body and the rock to work in unison. Again, he failed. As he straightened once again in frustration, he noticed that the eagle was no longer at his side. The eagle had moved to higher ground and was staring in awe at something emerging from the angry sea.

A large head had surfaced out of the water just off shore. It appeared like a sharp knife as it sliced through the water toward the island. As the shape of the huge creature emerged more clearly from the depths, its enormous body could now be seen clearly by the eagle and the monk.

Its massive size created a large wake despite the boiling torment of the waves. Its green eyes were set deeply in its imposing head, its mouth large and fierce. Several more heads, all smaller but equally ferocious-looking, rose out of the water behind the creature.

The large creature blinked the sea water from its piercing eyes, intently watching the eagle and the monk who now stood beside him. It stole ever more closely to the shore.

Nearing the shoreline, the giant creature raised itself fully from the water and made its way onto a rock at the shoreline. The skin of its head looked thick and hard and was layered as if it were armor. The green eyes were intense and clear. As its body became visible, the eagle and the monk saw an enormous, hard, glistening shell that resembled steel plates. The other creatures, many in number, surfaced near the shore. They floated in the rough water but didn't follow the leader ashore.

The huge tortoise climbed out of the water onto the rock and then stopped. It looked first at the tree, then moved its head from side to side, taking in the whole of the island with one sweep.

"Do you wish to harm us?" asked the monk haltingly, as the eagle spread his wings in a show of force and bravery.

"No," said the turtle, "quite the contrary. We come in friendship. Turtles are found all over the world and have no natural enemies. We live and let live.

"In many ancient lands, turtles have long been a symbol of tradition, of what should be maintained in the midst of change. I am the mother turtle. They call me sage."

The turtle turned her head first to the eagle, then to the monk.

"Eagle. Monk. I know of your dilemma. I know that you must find safety from this storm."

"That is true, sage, but we have nothing to work with. No tools," said the monk.

"Nor materials that will withstand this wind," added the eagle.

"But you have so much more than many others who have visited this island before you. You have come to understand and accept change. Even to welcome and seek it.

"And you believe in yourselves – and each recognizes the worth of the other. This is a fundamental lesson and a vital part of conquering change.

"Your belief in each other has been tested by adversity, and through this you have learned to trust each other—difficult for an eagle and a monk to do. But trust is the centerpiece, whether in the building of a nest or in any other worthy enterprise. Without trust, there can be little lasting success in such times of turbulence and change. It is a new kind of trust that you have learned—trust developed from and between very different traditions.

"Eagle, your trust was a trust created by rules and proven only when tasks were completed. This works well when the eagle in charge knows all. In the face of the constant winds of change, however, even eagle leaders cannot know all, see all, or command all for every situation. There will be too much change; too much of the world will be in transition. It will be impossible to construct a set of rules to cover every situation."

As she turned to the monk, the other turtles moved closer to better hear her words. "And you, monk, you have given your trust only to your group, to those similar to yourself. You cannot do this forever, because your group must now embrace many diverse people and many different beliefs if you are to survive. The winds of the world will demand, and deserve, a place to be heard, to be seen, and to be dealt with on their own terms. You have seen the power of their numbers.

"Whether you recognize it or not, you have become one with change. You now deal with change instinctively, freeing yourselves from the slow and tedious tasks of the old ways. Values guide your actions, not rules. Against a wind such as this, you need speed and flexibility," continued the turtle, "which you can now achieve with the ideas you have learned on this island."

"Thank you for your kind words," responded the eagle, "but as you can see, the wind destroyed our nest."

"And threatens to swamp our island," added the

monk. "Although we do not fear for our physical bodies, we think this wind is evil, as it never stops and never gives us any rest from its relentless force."

"The wind is not evil; it is but an agent of change," replied sage. "And the destruction of the nest is not important, for you learned much in its construction.

"I have watched you for many hours and am pleased with what I see. You have used your time on this island very well. You have learned many things and have added to your wisdom by coming to know each other's lives," explained the turtle.

"In earlier times, either of you could have found a way to survive with your special strengths. But in times of change, we must all constantly learn new ways. By learning the wisdom of each other, you have come very far."

Her final few words were barely heard by the eagle and the monk as a wave of force and violence swept over the turtle and crashed inches in front of them. The monk toppled over, and the eagle was swept several feet away. As they struggled to their feet, they saw the turtle retreating to the sea.

"Don't go! Come back!" they cried in unison, as the turtle slipped slowly into the sea. "Help us know what to do!"

Neither the eagle nor the monk heard the reply, "Seek the wisdom of the tree," as her words were carried out to sea by the sound of the waves crashing on the rocks.

8. The Wall

As the turtles sank from view, the wind suddenly slowed, and its heretofore ceaseless noise began to die down. Almost since they had first come to this island, the eagle and monk could now speak without shouting. By then, they had retreated back to the crevice in the rocks.

"I think she wanted us to try again to build the wall," said the monk as he snuggled into the crevice.

"Perhaps that is the best thing we can do," said the eagle, climbing in after him. "This calm is but the eye of the storm. We should use our time wisely now, as the wind will surely return with a vengeance."

"I know how to build a wall, eagle, but I do not have the strength to move these rocks. They are too heavy for such an old monk."

"We surely need help," said the eagle, "because my wings are not much good for moving rocks either.

"Did you notice that the turtle was not alone, that she had many others with her? Perhaps, perhaps . . ."

With that the eagle left the rocks and began circling the nearby waters in search of the sage. Fortunately for the eagle, whose wing was still not healed, he quickly saw a string of bubbles, then the flotilla of enormous shells just below the surface. Swimming in front was the sage. She was easy to spot because she had the largest and most scarred of the shells. Around her, the eagle counted dozens of turtles. The small group was headed toward the eastern horizon, in a vast sea that seemed to go on forever with no land visible in any direction.

Dropping close to the surface of the water slightly in front of the sage, the eagle swooped down several times until the old sage took notice. On seeing the eagle, she stopped almost immediately, and as if by silent communication, the rest of the turtles stopped as well.

"Back so soon to seek my guidance," she said as her head broached the water.

"Yes," said the eagle, "and to ask your help, or at least the help of your 'flock' — is that what you call a group of turtles?"

"We call a group of turtles a bale, and unlike eagles, we like to group together on occasion. But that is another story. What do you want from us?"

"The monk and I have decided to build a wall on the island, but neither of us has the ability to do so. I came to ask for the help of your turtles."

"I will have to ask them, but I can assure you they will be anxious to help. However, they do not know how to build a wall. Turtles swim free and have no need of walls."

"Fortunately, the monk is a master craftsman, and while he has never built a wall, he knows how to build things. I will help by watching from above. I think we have little time left, as I feel the return of the storm."

"We feel it too, eagle. That's why we were leaving as fast as turtles can go. We are from the land of a billion people, and it was their breath that created the wind that destroyed your nest.

"However, there are many more lands to the east and the south and even to the north and the west. Each has the power to create such a wind, and each will be strong and unique in its own way. And, they wait impatiently for their turn to blow," explained the turtle.

"Although the wind from my homeland was very new and very strong, and certainly strange to both you and the monk, the wind that comes now will be strange even to me. I can offer help and guidance but no guarantees. I have a premonition that this wall is not the answer."

"At this point it is our only viable solution. We expect no guarantees. We seek only your wisdom and the strength of your turtles."

The old she-turtle submerged to confer with her bale. They spoke to her of the need to help the eagle and the monk. Nodding her agreement after many thoughtful moments, the old turtle surfaced and headed back to the island. The eagle flew ahead to alert the monk. As she neared the island once again, the sage felt a strange new wind, blowing from a new direction, seductively caressing, then suddenly chilling her shell. She sensed it was a warning that her time had come.

The monk was ready when the turtles came ashore. He quickly organized them into small teams and put them to work moving the rocks into place. Often one turtle could simply lift a rock in its mouth and move it as the monk directed. Other times, several turtles were needed to lever the rocks into place. The turtles had never before built a wall, but after the monk carefully described the task, the turtles completed it.

The construction proceeded rapidly. Sage, too old to work, sat upon the largest rock. She told the story of her life as the work progressed. The turtles and the monk found the story a soothing antidote to the hard labor of wall building.

The eagle wished he could hear the turtle better, but he heard only pieces of the story as he circled overhead, shouting encouragement and offering essential guidance from his vantage point in the air. He struggled against the increasing force of the wind, which was now blowing harder by the minute.

The monk found the eagle's help from the air invaluable, but soon the eagle had to land because of the increasing force and noise of the wind. The sage was near the end of her story, but no one heard her final words over the noise of the wind.

The waves were once again threatening to swamp the island as the last rocks were fitted into place.

The turtles needed to seek the safety of the deeper water, and they turned to leave. The sage watched while each made its way to safety, waiting for the last to leave.

Turning to the monk she said, "This is a very fine wall indeed. The rocks are fitted as if they were placed there by nature."

"Thank you, mother turtle," said the monk. "I have always believed that a good craftsman leaves no traces of the work."

With that the eagle and the monk made their way behind the wall, and the turtle turned to look toward the sea. She did not follow the other turtles, though, stopping instead in front of the wall, unseen by the eagle and the monk.

As they settled into the narrow space behind the wall, the monk looked to the eagle and said, "A wall such as this will protect us from the wind and the sea. However, it is not perfect, and I must study ways to make it so. Perhaps we can remove some of the smaller stones to allow a little of the water to come through, lessening its force against the wall."

"That would be a waste of precious energy," responded the eagle. "There is no way to build a wall against the outside. This wind is too powerful! Feel it encircle the wall. Do you not feel its power through every crack, and over the top, and around the sides!"

"Yes, I feel its power, but at least we can now hear ourselves talk," said the monk.

"I agree, monk, so I will tell you what is on my mind while you can hear me."

For several minutes, the eagle looked up at the wall the monk had made, then twisted around to face him.

"Perhaps at one time, walls could keep out the rest of the world, but not today and certainly not tomorrow. We must find ways to use this wind to our advantage, to work with it, not against it," argued the eagle. "This wall is but a temporary shelter."

"I believe this is one of the great lessons of our times: No one can build a wall against the rest of the world," explained the eagle. "I don't know why you wish to build walls. Monks have always been able to change and adapt, to take the best that others have to offer and make it work for monks. Why do you need a wall, when monks have become so powerful, so skilled at change?"

"You must understand," replied the monk, "that our resistance to change is very great. We do not like change at all. When change comes, it comes slowly, and we study the process of change as much as the change itself.

"Yes, we have become used to change, but like everything else, we have our special way of doing so," explained the monk. "Walls give us time to think, to plan, and to slowly change. For monks, change must be gradual and well thought out. We call it *kaizen*. We dislike radical change. It is hard for monks who revere tradition.

The monk continued, "But we do embrace small changes that can lead us to perfection. At our temples, we cultivate trees to be like the one on this island. We carefully prune their leaves and branches every year, but we do so according to a plan that covers many hundreds of years.

"Each monk's role in the pruning, which covers one lifetime, is insignificant in attaining the final goal of a perfect tree. This is a goal that we can only see in our minds but never see in reality, because it may take the lifetimes of a dozen or more monks to achieve. Therefore, each individual monk must be satisfied with perfecting his small part, for the greater good of a perfect tree and for the good of all monks.

"Each monk is encouraged to suggest to his group— his order of monks—how to make small, incremental changes that help improve the process of pruning, but he and his order understand that they cannot change the pruning plan.

"And certainly no monk would suggest a change that would upset the *wa*, the harmony of his group. To create such disorder would bring great shame to him and his group—the very worst offense. Such a situation is unthinkable. Changes suggested from outsiders are almost always rejected," said the monk with great passion. "These are the ways of the monk."

"Ha! Eagles also resist change! Sometimes more than you monks. I know few eagles that enjoy change, although many preach its virtues in our councils," the eagle said, almost laughing. "To us eagles, your ways of dealing with change seem very slow, secretive, and insular. For eagles, change is dramatic and revolutionary. Often, change is so revolutionary that it requires a great leader with lots of power to accomplish it.

"But I must also admit that we eagles often change for the sake of change, to impress others with an appearance of progress. That's why the eagles give special names to change. In eagle-speak, we might call such changes 'refeathering' and 'total nesting management,' or TNM as we came to call it," said the eagle, now enjoying himself immensely at the thought. He named several more of these changes and translated them from 'eagle-speak' for the benefit of the monk.

"We seem to find a new one every couple of months or so. At least that's what most of the eagles think. These eagles have caught on to the trick, and they often resist such changes. Despite the clever names for change, eagles resist them to protect their own nests. They often believe that such changes are forced on them only for the benefit of the eagles in charge."

With that the monk could not resist, and he protested. "But some of those ideas have worked for monks. In fact, some of them came originally from eagles. We enhanced and perfected them and gave them back to you. We know they work!"

"Maybe for monks," said the eagle, "but eagles are not monks!"

"For eagles, we must see the goal to understand our individual role and to know how each eagle, especially the eagles at the top of the tree, will profit from the change. We are driven by our eagleness, just as you are driven by the essence of being a monk. When eagles fail to change, it is because we fear failure," admitted the eagle. "We know that . . ."

The wind began to wail louder now, and the monk could no longer hear even the piercing voice of the eagle.

The wind was growing stronger, stronger than either believed it could, and the rocks atop the crevice began to shift slightly under the pressure of the wind and the rising water.

The wall had been built to face the wind from the east. As the eagle and the monk shifted themselves to be even deeper into the crevice, they felt the wind shift direction, slightly at first and then with an unbelievable force. It shook the wall so strongly that several of the rocks, despite their solid placement, began to fall. The wall withheld the first assault, but then the wind changed again and again and again, switching direction every couple of minutes.

Despite the battering, they thought their wall would hold. Then, a huge wave of water, whipped into a frenzy by the wind, crashed savagely into the side of the wall. The rocks started to tumble in toward them. They scrambled out from behind the wall in time to see the rest of the rocks fall into the crevice. The rocks were followed by another huge wave that filled the crevice completely.

As they watched in horror, the water crashed with such power on the rocks that they knew they had escaped certain demise by a few seconds. They also realized that the next time they might not be so lucky.

As they stared in disbelief at the water-filled crevice, they heard a faint moaning from the front of the wall. Struggling in the direction of the noise, they found the old turtle beneath the rubble. Pushing the rocks away as best he could, the monk eased the pressure on the turtle.

As the eagle peered closer, he could see the shell of the old turtle had cracked in many places.

"Sage, what have we done to you!" cried the eagle. The monk bowed his head as if in silent prayer.

"You have done nothing to me, eagle, nor you monk. This was my fate. It was prophesied. My death does not take me by surprise—I have always been ready to go. I weep not for myself. You should not weep for me either."

"But sage, sage . . ." whispered the monk, close now to the old turtle's head.

"Enough," said the turtle, "I am dying and must soon return to the water. I need to say some more things to you before I go, things I think you will now understand."

9. The Tree

"Listen to my words," said the old turtle weakly. "I have had many years on land and at sea. I will tell you now the wisdom I have learned."

"You have made much progress, eagle, and you too, monk. Importantly you have learned to listen to each other and to those like my brother turtles who have worked for you. It is most important that you have learned to listen to those around you. In a time of great winds of change, no one, no matter how powerful, can know everything. Great leaders listen, and listen closely." The monk and the eagle leaned closer and strained to hear the words she spoke.

"I am pleased that you have come to this island, to be with me at the end. You were selected because you had been tested many times and never found wanting.

"This is a strange time for you both. We are most certainly in a period of change unlike any for many thousands of years. In my homeland I have often heard the wind curse: May you live in interesting times. You will surely live that curse, because change has now become permanent—the norm, not the exception.

"With the belief in both the worth of the individual and the value of the team, cemented together firmly by real trust, change becomes not the enemy but an ally.

"In fact, change becomes a positive thing. Cherished. Used to advantage. When there is no change from external forces, change is created by those closest to the task at hand. Change becomes not something to overcome, but a strategy for success.

"You must value the power of both individuals and groups, but above all, you must trust. Trust liberates decision-making and unleashes the power of both the individual and the group. You have worked together well, each in turn, as a champion and as a master, bringing your unique skills to bear at the right times. And you found me, the sage, to remind you of this. Now, you must seek the wisdom of the tree."

"The tree?" said the eagle.

"Does it hold the answer to our being here, to our fate?" interjected the monk.

"Let me rest a minute," replied the turtle, before they could ask her more. "Think of what you have learned since you first rested in the shade of the tree and refreshed your bodies with its fruit."

The turtle grew silent then as a sudden gust of wind blew through the few remaining branches of the tree, creating a loud rustling sound and reminding them all that change really is a permanent part of existence. The monk went to speak, but the eagle held up his injured wing as if to slow him.

"Let me rest, please. It is growing dark," the old turtle gasped, her breathing heavy and labored.

As suddenly as the wind had turned to anger and fury, it again, just as suddenly, lost its strength. In fact, the wind was now calm, a gentle breeze that seemed to create a peace and contentment they had not known since before their meeting.

The island had been their home for only a short time, but each realized he had gained a lifetime's worth of knowledge. Now each in his own way wanted to reflect on his experience and what it meant for the future.

Maybe, as the turtle had told them, they were chosen because they had been tested many times — singled out because of their ability to see beyond the immediate, to take a longer view, and to understand what had happened to them in their respective lives.

Maybe it was preordained by some great power.

Maybe they were supposed to be here, to be challenged, to be tested, to have the very essence of their
beliefs put into question, and, most importantly, to
struggle to find a new way to meet the future.

And the tree—what a decisive role it had played in
their experience! How could they explain the tree?

It was the monk who spoke first, just as he did when
they met at the tree.

"Eagle, my friend, mother turtle, our sage, is right. It
is time we speak of those things that I know have troubled you greatly, as they have troubled me. Everything
happened so suddenly—I am still not sure what to make
of it all!" said the monk, lowering his head just slightly.
"Our experience on this island has challenged so much
of what I held sacred. I hope I can be open enough to
deal with it!"

The eagle looked at them but didn't speak for many
minutes. Then he spoke in a tone and manner that mir-
rored those of the monk.

"Many have argued, both monks and eagles, that we
are competitors, that we are even enemies. But in your
tradition, and also in mine, there is a strong belief that
we have much in common and that our futures will
share even more in common. I believe this, monk."

The eagle paused momentarily, then continued.
"Certainly there will be times when we will be on
different sides of an issue. We'll be fierce competitors,
but this does not mean we have nothing to share with
one another. You called me friend, and I now call you

the same, friend. We have learned much together on this island, and we both owe much to the tree for its guidance.

"You are not the only one who has to rethink much of what you held to be the truth, the way to success. I also have much to consider . . ."

"The wind is both a blessing and a curse," interjected the monk. "It has created a new world for us both! I believe there are many more such winds of change to come, some as powerful as this one, others with less power. But all will have just as much potential to create change, because they will come from different traditions, with ideas different than either yours or mine.

"And, they will come from the north and the south, from the east and the west, and from all places in between," said the monk. "We will know little of their coming until they arrive. They will study us carefully and then use our strengths against us while adding new strengths of their own. We will need to be flexible and work like we've never worked before—certainly harder, but mostly smarter!"

The monk closed his eyes in contemplation, then added, "In this new world of many winds, each monk and every eagle will be called on not just for their brawn but for their brains as well."

"This is true, monk," said the eagle. "But we have much ground to cover with both those who command and those who follow—both monks and eagles. There have been many centuries of doing things the same way, but I fear this is no longer the case. Too much is changing, and changing so fast!"

"But I've learned much from you, the turtle, and the island," said the monk, "Much that I want to tell the other monks. I will be a 'champion,' as the turtle called it, for this new way."

"The eagles, too, must hear of this. I will be a leader in talking about this new way—this way of true empowerment," said the eagle. "Tell me, monk, how do you think we should begin? What shall we say?"

The monk replied, "I will start first with this idea of the worthiness of the individual—everything starts there. Although monks accept the dignity of the individual, it is the group that is more important. Perhaps I can show them the power of the individual to learn and bring diverse talents to any task. Do you not agree, eagle?"

The eagle looked out on the now calm blue-green waters that encircled their island. He hesitated a moment before answering the monk.

"In my land, the land of the eagles, the individual has been the foundation of eagle society for many hundreds of years. It started with our great eagle ancestors across the ocean, the lands that gave us many of our traditions. The sanctity of the individual was a lesson we came to cherish after centuries of conflict and turmoil. There are those who argue politically about the need to consider the larger community, but no one seriously questions the dignity and supremacy of individual eagles.

"And, I must admit, we have eagles, and then we have eagles. Some eagles are thought to be more important because of the size and shape of their feathers, or because they are man-eagles. With such a wind as we have seen, we can no longer afford to make such distinctions. And because of this, monk, I think that I will begin my story with the power of the group," explained the eagle. "Also, I will tell them we will no longer need to spend so much energy and time on command and control, the very essence of the eagle style, if there is real trust between those who work and those who lead.

"But, monk, we still need leaders . . ."

"I agree wholeheartedly," responded the monk. "But with this new way that we're discussing, leaders and leadership will be quite different for monks and, I suspect, for eagles, too."

The monk held up his hand as if to ask for a brief moment of silence, then he, like the eagle before him, looked out over the tranquil waters.

He turned his head sharply around, as the turtle again spoke in her hushed tones.

"Leaders will become masters of the overall strategy, creating teams by understanding the unique strengths and capabilities of individuals. Leaders will trust each member to contribute and will not command and supervise each move. They will rely on team discipline to get the job done.

"But even leaders need help!" said the turtle. "We must also have champions—guardians of the overall vision—whose role is to create the spirit of winning from within. They are champions of the task at hand, and they inspire others with their passion for the team, the task, and the accomplishment of something important.

"As you have found here on this island, the champion of one task need not be the champion of every other task. Any individual may rise to the challenge and take on the role of champion because of a particular interest or skill."

The eagle majestically nodded his concurrence, and the monk acknowledged the words with a serene smile.

Lifting her old head with difficulty, the turtle continued: "I know that much of this has been difficult for you both, and I can sense that each of you still has some reservations. I know you do not wish to throw away important parts of your heritage. You want to keep monks monks, and eagles eagles. And so you should.

"You, eagle, have learned much and changed for the better. But never forget what made you an eagle. And you, monk, have learned and changed as well. All monks will profit from your message. But understand, too, that you are a monk, and you must preserve the special qualities of being a monk while growing to accept a new way.

"In fact, my role as a sage is to guard and protect the culture, to help bridge the gap between old and new. Sages are critical in times of such accelerated change, because they can stay above the fray and add perspective and continuity.

"Sages are also important, because they provide wisdom while so many others simply provide information. Sages absorb all of history to become wise. A great sage once posed the question, 'Who is wise?' The answer: 'One who can learn from every person.' Thus, any monk or eagle can achieve this wisdom.

"My role as a sage is also to remind you to take the time to celebrate and reward the accomplishments of individuals and to encourage common sense for the common good.

"You have learned well about the changes of the past century. They will be the accepted wisdom of the next century. Now you must act, if you wish to tell others of these things . . ."

"But how? What?" said the monk.

"Seek the wisdom of the tree . . ." said the turtle as she shut her eyes for the final time.

"We must do as she says and seek the wisdom of the tree," said the eagle, "but first we must return the turtle to the sea."

"It is as she wished," responded the monk as he pushed her off the rock and into the sea.

Just above the surface of the water, many green eyes watched in silence as the old turtle slipped from view. Quickly, they too were gone from sight.

Then one head rose out of the water and called to the eagle and the monk as they looked out to sea.

"Eagle. Monk. I am the new sage. Although not as old as the mother turtle, I have stayed close to her side and learned her ways. The other turtles will now look to me for guidance. This is our way.

"While we cannot tell you more, the mother turtle told me of your dilemma. I know that you must leave this island. In earlier times, either of you could have found a way to do so with your special strengths. But in times of change, we must all constantly learn new ways. Seek the wisdom of the tree now, and you will learn to do so."

Suddenly the wind rustled the leaves of the tree again. This time, however, it was with renewed force. It suddenly engulfed the island with its power and with each passing moment became stronger. It seemed to be saying:

"Enough of this talk. It's time to go back to the real world to see what you've really learned from all this. And I will test you!!!"

Within seconds, the wind had returned to its earlier strength. It once again forced the waters to boil in torment and to crash wildly on the island. Again it came from many directions at once, swirling around the island and rocking the tree backward and forward, side to side. The tree creaked under the force of the wind, and it appeared that it could snap at any moment.

"Two things are clear, monk," said the eagle. "First, we can stay no longer on this island. The wind is causing the water to rise, and the island will soon be covered.

"Second, an eagle as powerful as me might be able to fly a short distance against this wind, but could not go far. With my injured wing I know I cannot fly from this island. There is not enough time for my wing to heal. We need to leave, monk, you and I, and we need to find a way to do this together."

"Then let us seek the wisdom of the tree," said the monk. "Perhaps it will offer some guidance."

As they approached the tree that had offered them refuge, they noticed for the first time that it was not as perfect as they had originally thought. They looked at the limbs badly damaged by the storm and then began to notice that its bark was not as straight, clean, and true as they had seen that first day. The leaves were still green but were not as perfect in shape and form and strength as they had thought when building their nest. They tasted the fruit, and while still good, it did not fill and satisfy them as they remembered.

"I saw this tree as perfect in every detail, never changing, a constant in the events that were swirling around me," said the monk.

"I did as well," said the eagle. "It drew me to this island with its beauty. I felt it a perfect tree for an eagle. Now I see that it is a good tree, but not a perfect one. It too has changed, or at least I see it more clearly now for what it is. Its wisdom is that all must change, even that which we see as perfect."

"This is the first great lesson," added the monk.

Neither the eagle nor the monk had any doubt that his time on the island was indeed over. This time there was no need for words, as the silent look between them said it all.

The eagle broke the silence. "I have always trusted only myself, but I now also trust you."

The monk responded in turn. "We may fail yet again, eagle, but we should never give up trying."

They knew they needed no more talk between them. They had to move, and move quickly, to put into practice the many lessons they had learned—lessons that would help them survive.

Standing several feet apart at the base of the tree, they turned together to look at the spot where the turtle had returned to the water, then paused only briefly to glance at each other—an unlikely pair from such different traditions.

At that very moment, finally succumbing to the constant torment of the wind, the huge tree snapped with a shudder and crack and fell between them, shaking the ground violently. The eagle and the monk began to move in unison . . .

Endnote

Our story is told.

Now, you the reader must ask yourself, would you be able to get off the island?

Can you grow and learn like the eagle and the monk?

As students of both individual initiative and organizational success, the authors believe that the moral of our story is:

Truly successful individuals and organizations of the future will embrace change by combining the best of Eastern traditions and Western traditions into the Seven Principles of Successful Change.

Expanding the Seven Principles of Successful Change

Accept Your Worth, Acknowledge Others' Worth

Every person has worth, including you. Accept your worth and acknowledge the worth of others around you. Accepting and acknowledging worth is the foundation of successful change.

- Everything starts with the acknowledgment of one's own worth, the worth of others, and of every living thing.
- Each individual is born with the ability to contribute and bring unique and diverse talents to the world.
- Without the belief that every person has worth, there is no foundation on which to build a relationship.
- Worth is critical to all people — in their private lives as members of families and social organizations and in their professional lives as members of groups, teams, and larger organizations.
- When worth is truly recognized, tasks become much more meaningful to the individual, and personal and organizational productivity increases dramatically.
- Self-worth is the foundation of life. Without the belief that you have worth, it is difficult, if not impossible, to develop your full potential as a human being.

Generate Trust

When there is trust between two or more people, change is more readily accepted. Being trusted and trusting others allows you and others to be positive, productive individuals. Trust is a centerpiece of successful change.

- When trust is central in any organization, team, family, or relationship, the productivity level of the self and others is enhanced.
- Where trust is central, change is confronted by cooperation, consensus, and personal commitment.
- Concerns about mistakes are greatly diminished as trust creates tolerance.
- Serious failures are dealt with quickly as trust spurs collective corrective action rather than unproductive retribution.
- Generating trust in a relationship or an organization is central to successful change.

Learn by Empathy

Those who continuously learn about themselves, others, work, and life have a greater capacity for change. By observing others, broadening interests, and understanding different perspectives, you can gain an instinctive understanding about change. Connect to change by daily learning.

- Learning daily updates skills and prepares individuals and groups for change.
- Learning by its nature promotes communication between and among individuals.
- Learning more about each other facilitates trust.
- Future change will be based more on knowledge than control.
- An attitude of learning frees the mind to consider new options and understand what had been unknown.
- Learning is a prescription for mastering change because the more you learn, the better equipped you are to handle change.

Embrace Change

Change is inevitable and appears to be increasing at exponential rates. You can either resist change or accept it. Since your life is simply a series of changes, be of change.

- Change is the fundamental force of our times.
- Change affects virtually every aspect of life. We know of no one nor of any organization that has escaped change.
- Change can be harnessed in positive ways by those who come to understand and embrace it, rather than fight against it.
- You may not be able to control change, but you can control how you react to change.
- Much like the characters in the fable, we need to understand change, channel it, and even welcome it.
- Individuals and organizations that successfully and continuously change will be the ones that experience lasting success.

Unleash the Synergy

Team synergy is the result of two or more people valuing and trusting each other. When two or more people produce ideas, they ultimately make improvements that are significantly greater than would have been possible separately.

- Individuals make unique contributions. Synergy — where individuals work together as connected communities and groups — multiplies those efforts many times over.
- Change is sometimes so overpowering that individuals cannot deal with it alone. A group generates power and resilience to survive and succeed.
- Groups learn to improve through mutual critiques and through the continuous celebration of accomplishments — both individual and collective.
- Synergy is abated and enhanced by open communication and information sharing, and control is alleviated and ideally eliminated.
- Due to today's volume and speed of change, team synergy is critical to individual, group, or organizational success.

Discover Champions, Depend on Masters, Find a Sage

Effective change will be steered by more than a leader. The environment of change will eliminate autocratic supervision. Instead, it will seek champions, masters, and sages to foster change.

- The concept of leadership is transformed as supervision is supplanted.
- Leaders, while still paying primary attention to strategy and direction, are increasingly becoming preoccupied with group culture and celebration.
- Champions have an abiding passion for their work, their group, their organization, and their role in making them successful.
- Champions lead by example and unwavering enthusiasm. Highly regarded by their group members, they constantly rejuvenate the group and prepare others for the role of champion in other areas.
- Masters complete tasks without supervision due to developed skills. Such skills have been developed by continuous learning and commitment.
- Masters are a stabilizing influence in individual or organizational change.
- Often overlooked, but fundamental to success in an era of rapid change, the sage blends the old with the new,

protecting the valuable traditions of the group while eas-
ing the rugged path to new ways.

- Most necessary during times of change and instability, the
sage focuses positive action out of defeat and despair.
- Always open to the new, but respectful of the old, the sage
helps promote common sense for the common good,
turns information and knowledge into wisdom, and spurs
the group to celebrate individual and team contributions.

Liberate Decision-Making

Change resulting from one person's decisions rarely works. Share decision-making with those around you—empower them. Ownership in decisions promotes change.

- No one individual can, in today's environment of change, succeed alone.
- In an era of pervasive and unrelenting change, organizations and individuals need to grant authority and responsibility to those who know best how to do what needs to be done.
- Allowing individuals and groups to think freely and make significant decisions promotes change.
- One person does not hold answers for all. Answers are discovered collectively.

Continuing the Journey

The Eagle & the Monk stimulates immediate discussion about many critical issues both in our work and home lives. Many of our readers voiced strong opinions that they wanted more, or at least they wanted to discuss the struggles and insights that the eagle and monk experienced. Specifically, and almost to the person, they wanted to talk about how this fable and its characters pertain to their lives and those around them.

In considering our readers, we've identified three major groups—students who are interested in leadership, change, and empowerment issues; employees, including management, who are ready to break out of traditional and structural organizational pyramids; and individuals who are interested in enhancing their own personal lives.

The Student

The book was given to a class of M.B.A. candidates, as well as recent graduates, from a nationally-ranked business school to explore the issue of change. Student response to the book was overwhelming. As one student stated, "The fable was much more readable than other business books. I enjoyed the format of a parable and the necessity to extract and ponder meaning." Time and time again, students commented on the book's refreshing approach to presenting today's business philosophies—"The usual fact/information format puts one to sleep. The fable paints a picture in your mind, which makes the leadership lessons more interesting and memorable." Numerous students noted that the book would be an excellent alternative to the traditional textbooks currently being used by business schools to teach change, leadership, team building, and management. In comparing the two types of books, one student commented, that "instead of boring the readers with academic chit-chat, the authors use a tale to teach lessons." Since the book offered so many pertinent lessons, they argued that a way to reinforce these discoveries should be provided.

Employees and Management

When *The Eagle & the Monk* was given to various executives across the U.S. and the Asian Pacific, all commented on how the book differed from the typical management books currently available. The book offered leadership lessons that were, as one reader said, "Easy to see and easy to learn." Yet with its reading ease, readers also noted the unique manner by which the story's deep symbolism was used: "I read the book cover to cover three times. The symbolism was excellent. I look forward to seeing it in management training curriculums. Management facilitators, as well as individual readers, could study in greater detail the book's lessons through thought-provoking questions and applications." One reader said it best when he noted, "One of the great strengths of the book is that it explains change in a way that doesn't allow a reader to put up learning barriers."

Personal Development

Many readers told us that "this is much more than a business book. It's about life." People saw it in dealing with their marriage, a child with ADD (Attention Deficit Disorder), a cross-country move, a health emergency, and even a teenage romance. One executive, from a leading information technology corporation, felt so strongly about the book's personal applications that he stated, *"The Eagle & the Monk* needs to go from the living room to the boardroom, not the other way around."

STARTING THE DISCUSSION

There are a number of ways this book can be used to start a discussion about change—whether it be an important relationship, a family or your company.

- Discuss change through each of the characters and their responses: the eagle, the monk, the turtle, and the tree.
- Start with the seven principles of change. Evaluate how each one applies to you and your organization. Determine which principles give you the most difficulty and which you need to improve.
- Take only one change principle at a given session and fully explore how you compare to the actions of the eagle and the monk. This method could be used for your personal and professional time.
- Select a powerful message from the book and develop discussion questions. To clarify how to do this, we have included two passages from each of the chapters about its respective principle of change.

These are but a few ways you can start or continue the dialogue about change. Each of these suggestions needs to involve two or more people, and in many cases, a facilitator can greatly enhance the discussion.

Chapter 3: The Rock

"I could, and did, face all of life's challenges with a steady face."(p. 52)

1. Is your life a series of challenges and changes? How?
2. How do changes at work affect your home life and vis-a-vis?
3. Is more than a "steady face" needed to face future challenges? Explain.

"I understand now that I was not alone, nor am I alone here, in my fear of change."(p. 54)

1. How do you overcome the fear of change at home? At work?
2. Why do some people fear change less than others?
3. Can change be controlled? Can you control how you react to it? Explain your responses.

Chapter 4: The Island

"There is no way for me to do so."(p. 60)

1. Why did the monk lack confidence and self-worth? Do you ever find yourself answering a challenge similar to the way the monk responded? What do you do?
2. If the monk doubts his own worth, he will also have difficulty acknowledging others' worth. Do you agree with this statement? Why or why not?

"Each of these elements of nature made a meaningful contribution to the final result."(p. 61)

1. Do you recognize the contributions of others in your
   personal or work relationships? How?
2. Are your best relationships (at work, in marriage, or in
   friendship) related to mutual acceptance of the other's
   abilities? Why or why not?

Chapter 5: The Wind

"Trust is conditional and changes with circumstances."(p. 65)

1. Does the eagle's view of trust limit him in his relationships with others? Explain.
2. What is your view of trust? What about those closest to
   you?
3. If your ability to trust others is limited, how does that
   affect how you respond to change?

"Those who trust the most are in turn the most
trusted."(p. 66)

1. Is this quotation true in your workplace? Is it true in your
   personal relationships? Explain your responses.
2. Is change easier or more difficult when there is trust
   present? Explain.

Chapter 6: The Nest

"The synergy of individual strengths coupled with like-minded others is the special magic of a team. Hard to explain, beautiful to watch!"(p. 74)

1. Have you felt this synergy in a personal relationship? At work? Explain.
2. Working within a team can be difficult at times. What makes teamwork difficult? List the difficulties.
3. During a period of change within your company, to what extent would a team give you strength?

"We must celebrate both the individual and the group if we are to survive and succeed in a time of challenge and change."(p. 75)

1. During a time of change, sometimes celebrations of accomplishment are forgotten. Is this true for you? For your company?
2. Is the power of a team greater than the power of an individual? Explain.

Chapter 7: The Sage

"In many ancient lands, turtles have long been a symbol of tradition, of what should be maintained in the midst of change. I am the mother turtle. They call me sage."(p. 81)

1. Who are the sages in your company? What role do they play?
2. Have you ever worked for a company without a sage? What do you believe are the differences in a company's culture and profitability when a sage is present versus when a sage is not present?
3. A sage can usually be found in extended families. Is there a sage in your family? What does a sage provide a family? Explain.

"You have learned many things and have added to your wisdom by coming to know each other's lives."(p. 83)

1. Does learning help or hinder you when dealing with change? Describe.
2. When thinking about any relationship, how much does learning improve a relationship? Why?
3. Can learning help you react to change instinctively? Explain.

Chapter 8: The Wall

"But after the monk carefully described the task, the turtles completed it."(p. 88)

1. Can one person successfully make major changes? Why or why not?

2. How important is ownership in decision-making? In change? Explain your responses.
3. To what degree does your company delegate decision-making and task accomplishment to its employees?

"There is no way to build a wall against the outside."(p. 90)

1. Interpret this statement. What does it imply?
2. Isolationism can be applied not only in personal relationships, but also in companies. What areas within your company is isolationism practiced? Briefly describe.
3. Cite ways in which to successfully dissolve isolationist attitudes and practices within your personal life and within your company.

Chapter 9: The Tree

"In fact, change becomes a positive thing . . . . when there is no change from external forces, change is created by those closest to the task at hand."(p. 96)

1. When it comes to personal relationships, is most change positive in the long run? How about when it comes to your family and your employment? Share reflections.
2. In your company, where does most of the change start and evolve from? Is change more successful top-down or bottom-up? Why?

"Champions inspire others with the passion for the team, the task and the accomplishment of something important."(p.100)

1. Is a champion selfless in his or her work? How? Is that good or bad?
2. How does a champion vary his or her style when faced with various changes and challenges? Explain.

"The eagle and the monk began to move in unison. . . ."(p. 106)

1. As you face change, is it important that you move in unison with those who are also affected?
2. To effectively deal with change, what elements are the most critical? What were the most critical elements to the eagle and the monk?
3. How do you determine how you react to change?